THE Wrong Toilet AND OTHER DISASTERS

WRITTEN BY
ALEXA TEWKESBURY
ILLUSTRATED BY
ANNA-MARIA GLOVER

CWR

Published 2018 by CWR, Waverley Abbey House, Waverley Lane, Farnham, Surrey, GU9 8EP, UK. CWR is a Registered Charity – Number 294387 and a Limited Company registered in England – Registration Number 1990308.

For a list of National Distributors, visit cwr.org.uk/distributors
Concept development, editing, design and production by CWR
Illustrations by Anna-Maria Glover
Printed in the UK by Linney.
ISBN: 978-1-78259-928-9

Meet the family!

Sparky (Sabrina)

Mr Smart (Seb/Dad)

Mrs Smart (Stella/Mum)

Stanley

Sissy

THE BAGGS

Auntie Bella (Stella's twin sister)
The twins: Nat and Archie (aka 'the crinkly cousins')
Grandad Bagg (Stella and Auntie Bella's dad)

RESIDENTS OF PRIORY PARK

Miss Clatworthy
Her cats:
Monday, Tuesday
and Thursday

The Obis
Mr Obi
Mrs Obi
Baby Eric
Minnie,
the Chihuahua

STORY 1

Surprise, surprise!

'Bye-bye, then,' Mrs Smart called from the doorstep, with her little daughter, Sissy, hugged to her hip. She tried to sound cheerful as she added, 'See you again soon!'

'Spoons,' mumbled Sissy through a mouthful of thumb.

Sissy Smart had recently discovered that sucking her thumb felt 'cumbly' (that's 'comfy' to everyone else). She'd taken to doing it whenever there was nothing more interesting within reach to put in her mouth. The day before, Mrs Smart had found her sucking a sock that belonged to her big sister Sparky. The sock had a picture of an ice cream on it. Fortunately, Sparky wasn't wearing it at the time.

Auntie Bella started her car in the Smarts' driveway and Mrs Smart raised a hand to wave.

Sparky, who stood next to her on the doorstep, waved too. Her crinkly haired cousins, on the other hand, did not wave back. They didn't even look up. Nat and Archie had barely stepped outside the Smarts' house since their mum had dropped them off at Priory Park on Friday evening. It had rained the whole weekend. Now it was Sunday evening and they were being whisked home again, but all of a sudden the weather had dried up. There was even the hint of a sunbeam escaping from behind a cloud. Sparky's cousins were not amused.

'Bye, Nat! Bye, Archie!' called Sparky.

Neither crinkly head moved.

I would say that the next moment, Auntie Bella revved the engine and screeched away, except that the ground was really far too wet for anyone to be able to do any screeching. Not even Auntie Bella, who lived her entire life in a rush because she was always late. So, the next moment, Auntie Bella revved the engine and... slopped away. After she'd driven through the gateway and out of sight, Sparky, Sissy and Mrs Smart could still hear the car slopping its way along the road.

'Well...' said Mrs Smart. 'That was, erm... exhausting.'

'Sauce-tin,' said Sissy, who had removed her thumb from her mouth. She was now tired of being clamped to her mum's hip. So she squirmed and wriggled until Mrs Smart was forced to put her down. Mrs Smart tried to grab her hand – too late. The instant Sissy's feet, clad in nothing but her woolly tights, hit the ground, she toddled off the front step – and sat down.

In a puddle.

She grinned and giggled. 'Wet, Mummy,' she announced.

Mrs Smart closed her eyes. 'Do you know what?' she murmured. 'I'm almost glad I've got to go and teach tomorrow.'

Sparky blinked. '*Are* you?' she asked. 'Really? Only when you got home from school on Friday, you said you wished it was the holidays because this term had been far too long already.'

Mrs Smart sucked in a noisy breath through her nose. 'Did I? Did I, really? Well, that was a silly thing to say, wasn't it? After being cooped up here all weekend with your two miserable cousins, I'm beginning to think the school term hasn't been nearly long enough!'

Straightaway, her hands flew to her mouth. 'Oh, I'm sorry, Sparky, I didn't mean that. Nat and Archie aren't miserable, they're lovely. They're just...'

'That's all right,' Sparky interrupted. 'They were quite miserable.'

Mrs Smart's hands dropped from her mouth and landed on her hips. She took in another deep breath and let it out again loudly. Sparky thought she sounded like one of the Smarts' blow-up mattresses (the ones Nat and Archie slept on when they came to stay) – deflating.

'Right, then,' said Mrs Smart. 'Do you know what I need?'

'A cup of tea?' Sparky asked.

'Oh, more than just one, Sparky,' replied Mrs Smart. '*So* many more than just one!'

With that, she hoisted Sissy out of the puddle and, holding her at arm's length, carried the dripping toddler into the house.

'I'll put the kettle on,' said Sparky.

Mrs Smart was already on the way to the bathroom to help Sissy out of her wet clothes. She stopped at the foot of the stairs.

'Will you? Are you sure?' She looked concerned. Sissy kicked her feet, flicking a spray of muddy water onto Mrs Smart and the carpet.

'Mum,' said Sparky, 'I do know how to put the kettle on, you know.'

'Do you?'

'Of course I do. I do it at Grandad's all the time.'

'*Do* you?' Mrs Smart repeated.

'Yes, all the time. He let me boil an egg once, too.'

'Did he?'

'Yes,' answered Sparky. 'It went a bit wrong, but Grandad didn't mind.'

What Sparky didn't say was that it went a bit wrong because she'd tried to boil the egg in the kettle.

'You'd be surprised what Grandad lets me do in his kitchen,' she added.

'Hmm...' Mrs Smart nodded in a confused sort of way.

'Yes, I rather think I might be.'

Sparky looked at the floor. 'Mum, I really think you should take Sissy to the bathroom now. She's dripping all over the hall.'

Mrs Smart glanced down at the spatters on the carpet. 'Oh, my goodness, yes. I'll be five minutes. Don't make the tea – just boil the kettle.'

'I *could* make the tea...' Sparky began.

Mrs Smart was halfway up the stairs. '*Just* boil the kettle!'

Stanley appeared on the landing. He looked hot.

Mrs Smart trotted past him to the bathroom. 'All right, Stanley?' She pushed open the bathroom door and stood Sissy in the bath.

'Do I look all right?' asked Stanley.

'Not really,' said Sparky. She gazed up at her brother from the hall. 'But then, to be honest, you never do.'

'I'm boiling,' Stanley complained.

'You look it,' said Sparky. 'You've gone a bit of a beetroot-y colour.'

'Why are you boiling?' called Mrs Smart from the bathroom. 'It's not very warm. In fact, if anything, it's quite nippy.'

'Nimpy,' Sissy said. 'Nimpy, nimpy...'

'I've been trying to sort out my bedroom,' grumbled Stanley. 'It's always a tip after Nat and Archie have stayed in it. It's taken me ages.'

Sparky shook her head. 'It can't have taken ages. They've only just left.'

'Well, it feels like ages,' Stanley snapped. 'I can't move for blow-up mattresses in there. And it smells.'

'Oh,' said Sparky. 'That could be you, though.'

Stanley's eyebrows shot up, then down again so quickly they crashed together. **'I do *not* smell,'** he said.

Sparky wasn't convinced. 'Not as bad as Dad does when he gets home from work, anyway,' she conceded.

Mr Smart was a personal trainer. His job of helping other people to get fitter meant that he often arrived home hot and sweaty at the end of the day. And there was always a hot, sweaty smell that arrived home with him.

Mrs Smart appeared in the bathroom doorway. She held Sissy, who was now mud-free and wrapped in a towel.

'Did you say Dad was home?' she asked. 'Why's he home? He shouldn't be home yet. It's far too early. What's happened?'

'Dad's not home,' said Stanley.

Mrs Smart frowned. 'Then why did Sparky say he was?'

'I didn't,' said Sparky. 'I said Stanley doesn't smell as bad as Dad does when he gets home from work.'

Mrs Smart stepped towards Stanley and sniffed. 'That's very true, you know, you don't.' She sniffed again. 'Mind you,' she added, 'something smells a bit... odd.'

Stanley glared. 'That's not me! That's Nat and Archie! It's what they've left behind.'

Mrs Smart looked alarmed. 'Really? What *have* they left behind?'

Stanley threw up his hands. 'What do you think? Their smell!'

Mrs Smart glanced at Sissy who looked almost as puzzled as she did. 'Let's go and find you some clean clothes, Missy Sissy. Has the kettle boiled yet, Sparky?'

'Ooh!' said Sparky. 'I forgot to put it on.'

'Don't worry,' replied Mrs Smart. 'I'll be down in two ticks and I'll do it.'

'No, that's all right. I'll do it.'

'You really don't have to.'

'I really don't mind.'

'Fine,' said Mrs Smart. 'But be careful.' Then, 'Stanley,' she added, 'pop down to the kitchen, would you? Make sure Sparky doesn't electrocute herself with the kettle.'

'Mum, I'm trying to tidy my room,' Stanley moaned. 'And Sparky says I look like a beetroot.'

'Well, Sparky will look a lot worse than a beetroot if she electrocutes herself.' Mrs Smart turned and headed for Sparky and Sissy's bedroom. 'Hurry up, please, Stanley.'

Ten minutes later, Sparky, Stanley and Mrs Smart sat round the kitchen table. Sissy sat under the table and fed pretend carrots to a pink cuddly unicorn.

Mrs Smart stared at the mug of very dark brown, thick-looking tea in front of her.

'So, Stanley,' she said, 'exactly how many tea bags did you put in the pot?'

Stanley shrugged his shoulders. 'I didn't put in any, Sparky did. All I put in was the water.'

'I put in a lot of tea bags.' Sparky looked pleased with herself and beamed all over her face. 'A whole double handful so that must be at least... 20. Well, you said you wanted lots of cups.'

Mrs Smart nodded. 'I did say that, yes. It's just that, in the interests of conserving the world's tea supplies for future generations, just bear in mind that two to three bags is normally plenty for this pot.'

'But you're not feeling normal, are you?' replied

Sparky. 'You never feel normal after Nat and Archie have been to stay. So I thought you deserved more than normal tea. You deserve **super-tea**.'

'Well, thank you for the thought, Sparky,' Mrs Smart said. She hesitated as she continued to stare at the ominous-looking contents of her cup.

'Aren't you going to drink it?' asked Sparky.

'Yes, of course...' said Mrs Smart. 'In a little bit... Perhaps I'll have a drop more milk.'

She fetched a bottle from the fridge and splashed some more milk into the top of her mug. The mug was already full so there wasn't much room and the splash didn't make any difference to the colour of the tea. It was still a deep, earthy, muddy brown.

Stanley plonked his elbows on the table. 'Not that any of you have noticed, but *I* never feel normal after Nat and Archie have been to stay either. I'm the one whose space gets invaded. I'm the one who has to breathe in their smell all night long.'

'Yes,' said Sparky, 'but then they have to breathe in your smell all night long, too.'

'But there's two of them. That's twice the smell.'

'True,' agreed Sparky. 'But you're taller.'

Stanley glared. 'Well, I'll tell you something for nothing – when it's my birthday there's no way I'm inviting them to my party.'

'Stanley!' Mrs Smart frowned. 'That's a bit mean.'

Sparky frowned too. 'Since when have you ever had a birthday party?'

'Since...'

'You don't even like parties,' Sparky interrupted.

'Especially not for your birthday. It was all Mum and Dad could do to get you to come to *my* birthday party last year. And even then you only agreed because they said you could have a birthday cake too – all to yourself.'

'You mean an *un*birthday cake,' Stanley said.

'Pardon?'

'You mean an *un*birthday cake.'

Sparky blinked at him.

'Well, it couldn't be a birthday cake, could it?' Stanley reasoned. 'Because it was your birthday, not mine. So it must have been an *un*birthday cake.'

Sparky's eyes narrowed. 'Anyway,' she said, 'you only came to my birthday party because you had a whole something-or-other cake all to yourself. Not because of the games or the prizes or the music or the *fun*. That's how much you hate parties.'

'So?' Stanley sat back in his chair. 'All I'm saying is, when it's my birthday I'd rather spend it without Nat and Archie.'

'Well,' Sparky replied, folding her arms, 'perhaps Nat and Archie won't want to spend your birthday with you anyway.'

The next moment, both Sparky and Stanley almost jumped out of their skins. Sissy didn't. She was far too absorbed in pulling more pretend carrots up from the pretend earth to pretend to feed to her pink cuddly unicorn.

The reason for the jumping was a loud slapping sound – the sound of Mrs Smart bringing the palms of both hands down hard on the table and shooting up out of her seat.

Stanley and Sparky were so startled, they shot out of their seats too.

'What, Mum?' Sparky gasped.

'Birthdays!' wailed Mrs Smart. *'Birthdays!'*

Sparky and Stanley looked at each other in confusion. Sissy shoved yet another pretend carrot in her cuddly unicorn's face, scrunching up its shiny pink nose.

Mrs Smart threw her hands in the air. 'It's your dad's birthday!'

Sparky and Stanley's mouths dropped open for a moment. Then they both snapped shut.

'Mum,' said Sparky, 'it's not Dad's birthday.'

'Yes, it is!' insisted Mrs Smart.

'No, it's not, Mum,' said Stanley. 'Dad's birthday isn't till the thirtieth. Not unless he's moved it.'

Sparky's mouth dropped open again. 'Has Dad moved his birthday? What for? I didn't even know you could do that.'

'I don't know if he *has* done that.' Stanley shook his head. 'But if he has, it's a bit daft to move it and not tell us. How does he think he's going to get any presents?'

'He's obviously told Mum,' Sparky replied.

'Yes, and Mum's obviously forgotten,' said Stanley. 'Which isn't surprising really, considering she's used to his birthday being on the thirtieth, not the third like it is today.'

Mrs Smart glanced from Stanley to Sparky and back again. 'What are you talking about?'

'Dad moving his birthday,' answered Sparky. 'Isn't that what *you're* talking about?'

'No...' Mrs Smart looked mystified. 'Anyway, no one moves their birthday. I mean, what would be the point?' She dropped back down onto her chair.

Stanley and Sparky sat back down too.

'Exactly,' said Stanley. 'So why has Dad moved his birthday to today?'

'Stanley, Dad's birthday isn't today.'

'Then, why did you say it was?'

'I didn't!' Mrs Smart was growing more and more confused. So much so, that without thinking she grabbed her mug and took a big gulp of her thick, dark, earthy, mud-brown tea.

She spluttered and for a second, her nose – in fact, her entire face – became even more scrunched than Sissy's poor, pretend-carrot-stuffed unicorn.

It took several moments for her face to recover itself. 'It's not Dad's birthday today,' she managed at last. She looked more like she'd just swallowed thick, dark, earthy mud than mud-brown tea. 'But it will be in a few weeks.'

'So, what's the problem?' asked Stanley. 'A few weeks is plenty of time to buy a present.'

Mrs Smart shook her head. 'But I can't *just* buy him a present, can I? Not this time.'

'Why not?'

'Because it's not just *any* birthday. It's a special birthday. Dad's turning 40.'

Sparky made a face. 'Doesn't sound special to me. Sounds *really* old.'

'So, buy him a special present, Mum,' said Stanley. 'Something like...'

'A walking stick?' suggested Sparky. 'If Dad's 40, then pretty soon he's going to be needing a walking stick.'

Mrs Smart peered at her and wondered if her daughter was joking. 'Sparky, Dad does not need a walking stick. He's 40, not 140! But the thing is, people do things when they're turning 40.'

'Do they?' asked Sparky. She wondered what a 40-year-old person might be able to manage. 'Like what?'

'I don't really know,' answered Mrs Smart. 'Well, they have parties. Important fortieth birthday parties... I think.'

Stanley shrugged his shoulders. 'You don't need to worry, then. Dad hates parties.'

'He doesn't hate them,' replied Mrs Smart. 'He just

doesn't really go to any.'

'Because he hates them,' said Stanley.

Mrs Smart sighed. 'Well, whether he hates them or not, he's going to have one. Because that's what you do when you turn 40.'

Stanley leaned back in his chair. 'Mum, you do know that's daft, don't you?'

'No, it's not. Dad'll love it, you'll see – because we'll have organised it for him.'

'"We"? What's this "we" business?' Stanley's eyebrows did a wiggle.

'Well, I can't do it all on my own. And it's got to be a complete surprise.'

Stanley blinked. 'Wait... what?'

'A surprise party?' Sparky's face beamed. '**Cool!**'

'No!' said Stanley. '*Not* cool! Do you know what Dad hates more than parties? Surprises! Don't you remember what happened when we went on that surprise boat trip with Grandad last year? All Dad kept saying was, "I wish I'd known. I love boats and all that – but I wish I'd known."'

'I'm not listening, Stanley,' said Mrs Smart. 'Dad's going to have a surprise fortieth birthday party, all organised by us, to show him how much we love him. And not a word to Dad – you've got to promise. If it's going to be a surprise, let's make it a *real* surprise!'

'Don't worry, Mum,' said Sparky, 'we won't say a word, will we, Stanley? Not even if Dad tortures us.'

Stanley wrinkled his nose. 'The only person who's going to end up being tortured is Dad – because he hates parties and he hates surprises.'

Mrs Smart got to her feet and picked up her mug.

'Actually, do you know what? I think I've let my tea get a bit cold. I'll make some fresh.'

'No need, Mum,' said Sparky, 'there's still a whole pot full.' She pushed the pot of tea, weighed down by its 20 plus tea bags, towards her.

Mrs Smart forced a weak smile. 'Oh, yes, so there is,' she replied. 'Lucky me.'

* * * *

One evening later that week, Sparky asked, 'Mum, have you decided what to do for Dad's surprise birthday party yet?'

'No,' Mrs Smart answered. 'I mean, when have I had the chance, Sparky? I've been at school every day and had marking to do every evening. I shan't have time to think about it till at least the weekend. This really is turning into *such* a long term.'

Sparky had been a Smart long enough to know that as soon as Mrs Smart mentioned what a long term she was having, it was best to slip quietly away. To ask any more questions was certainly not advisable. Not unless you wanted to bring on a twitch of Mrs Smart's eye – a sure sign that some sort of explosion was imminent.

'Right,' said Sparky. 'No problem.'

With that, she scampered upstairs and knocked on Stanley's door.

'What is it now?' Stanley grunted the question through the closed door as if he'd already been interrupted at least five times since he'd got home from school. He hadn't. He'd been shut away in his room, undisturbed, while he studied the long-range weather forecast on his laptop.

Stanley's dream was to become a TV weather person. He liked nothing better than to gather weather facts and astonish people with his weather knowledge. And he could present a pretty good forecast when he put his mind to it.

Sparky knocked on his door again. There was a moment's silence before it was suddenly whipped open.

'What?' Stanley demanded.

'I need to speak to you,' said Sparky. 'It's important.'

'I'm studying the long-range weather forecast. What could be more important than that?'

'Erm... nearly everything?' replied Sparky.

'You won't say that next time I save you from getting caught out at the park in a huge thunderstorm because I know exactly when it's going to arrive and you don't.'

Sparky thought there might be some truth in this, but she didn't say so. Instead she said, 'We need to talk about' – she leaned in towards Stanley and dropped her voice to a whisper – 'Dad's surprise fortieth birthday party.'

'Oh,' answered Stanley. 'You mean the surprise fortieth birthday party Dad's not going to want.'

'Yes, that's the one,' whispered Sparky.

Stanley stared at her. 'And why are you whispering? Dad isn't even home.'

'Isn't it obvious?' Sparky made a tutting sound with her tongue. 'I'm practising for when he *is* at home. Mum made us promise not to spoil the surprise, remember? So can I come in or not?'

Stanley heaved a sigh and, with a pained expression on his face, he stood back to let Sparky into his room. She plonked herself down on his bed.

'The thing is, Stanley, we need an idea.'

'What for?' Stanley asked.

Sparky rolled her eyes. 'What do you think? For Dad's party, of course.'

'I thought that *was* the idea. A party – we organise it; we go to it; we leave.'

'Yes, but what sort of party, Stanley? That's the big question.'

Stanley let out another sigh. This sigh was even deeper than the first. So deep and so heavy that Sparky was sure she saw Stanley's fringe lift slightly in the blast of gloomy air.

'It doesn't matter what sort of party it is,' he said. 'Dad still won't want it.'

'You say that now, Stanley,' Sparky replied. 'But what if it was a really interesting sort of party? You know – the sort of interesting party that you or I might have.'

'That just you might have, you mean. I don't do birthday parties, remember?'

'Oh, come on, Stanley,' Sparky moaned. Sometimes Stanley's lack of interest in anything but the weather was infuriating. 'If we can come up with a brilliant and extremely interesting idea for Dad's birthday party, then Mum won't have to. And you know what that means, don't you?'

'Do I?' muttered Stanley.

'Yes!' snapped Sparky. 'It means saving the hundred-or-so eye twitches Mum'll have when she realises she doesn't have time to think about it!'

Stanley pondered for a moment. Then he nodded his head. 'That is a good point,' he said. 'All right, then, here's an idea...'

'Yes?' Sparky gazed at her brother with eager eyes.

'Next time you see Grandad, ask *him*. Now, if it's all right with you, I'd like to get back to my long-range weather forecast.'

* * * *

Sometimes Sparky felt that being the only quick-thinking Smart on Priory Park was a bit too much of a responsibility. Especially when it came to something as important as Mr Smart's fortieth birthday.

'Grandad?' Sparky said, as she walked home from school with Grandad Bagg the next day. 'If you were going to organise a surprise birthday party for someone, what sort of thing would you do?'

Grandad thought for a moment. 'Well,' he replied, 'I suppose it would depend on who the surprise birthday party was for.'

'Oh.' Sparky hesitated. She couldn't tell Grandad that the party was for Mr Smart. She and Stanley had promised to keep it a secret. 'Erm... someone special who's having a special birthday.'

'Someone special, eh?' said Grandad.

'Yes. Someone very special. Someone like...' Sparky's quick-thinking brain whirred into action. '**God!**'

Grandad's bushy eyebrows slid halfway up his forehead. 'Someone like God, eh? Well, that must be someone very special indeed.'

Sparky nodded. 'Yes, it must. Someone we care about – like God. Someone we love. Someone who loves us back and does lots of kind things for us. Someone we just couldn't ever imagine living without.'

'Well, that's true enough,' said Grandad. 'I couldn't imagine living without God in my life. Not for a single second. I'd be lost.'

'Yes,' replied Sparky, 'so would I. And when you know you'd be lost without someone, you'd want to give them the most special-est party in the whole world, wouldn't you? So, what would you do?'

Once again, Grandad wore his thoughtful face. 'If it was a party for God, I'd sing to Him. I'd sing to God to tell Him how wonderful He is. Just like I sing to my tomatoes.'

Sparky pictured Grandad in their lounge, mouth wide open, singing his heart out to Mr Smart. She also tried to picture Mr Smart's face as he listened, sitting on the sofa with a huge slab of birthday cake that was far too big for the plate.

No... she thought. *Grandad's singing is* definitely *special. But somehow, I think God and Grandad's tomatoes will appreciate it more than Dad will.*

Obviously she didn't want to say this to Grandad. Instead she said, 'Hmm, singing. That's a brilliant idea. And what else?'

'What else?' repeated Grandad. 'Don't you think my singing's enough?'

'Oh, yes, of course! Your singing would be enough for anyone. Especially God. I'm sure He'd love it. And you're welcome to sing to me when it's *my* birthday. It's just that you might not be able to sing for a whole party. So it'd be good if there were other things to do as well – you know, to have "up our sleeves" as you sometimes say.'

They turned in through Grandad's front gate and Grandad fished his front door key out of his pocket.

'I've got an idea,' he said. 'We'll consult Beryl. Beryl will have lots of suggestions for a special birthday party.'

'Brilliant, Grandad!' Sparky's eyes shone. 'Why didn't I think of that? Of course she will!'

You're probably wondering who Beryl is and whether she can really come up with better ideas than Sparky. (Let's face it, not many can.) But the thing is, Beryl isn't a person. Beryl is Grandad's computer.

Now, it might seem unusual to give a computer a name. Grandad, however, had his reasons. He used to get very cross with his old computer when it wasn't working properly. (It's hard to imagine Grandad Bagg ever being cross, but sometimes he'd even shout at his computer, and Grandad Bagg never shouted at anything.) So, when he finally bought a new one, he thought that if he gave it a name, it might seem less like a computer and more like a good friend. And if it was more like a friend, then he was far less likely to shout at it when it was being silly.

Beryl whirred and ticked into life. When she was ready, Grandad typed in his request: *Ideas for a special birthday party, please.* Almost at once, a long list of possibilities popped onto the screen. He scrolled down and clicked on one.

'What's a themed party?' asked Sparky.

'It's where everyone goes dressed up as something,' Grandad replied.

'You mean, if it was a monster theme, everyone could dress up as monsters?'

'Something like that. Or if it was a French theme, all the food might be from France.'

Sparky had a think. She quite liked the idea of dressing

up as a monster, but she wasn't sure how Mr Smart would feel about it. And if the French food happened to be unhealthy, Mr Smart probably wouldn't enjoy it. Not only was he a personal trainer who helped people to get fit on the outside, he also wanted them to get fit on the inside. This meant that, in their family, they ate a lot of vegetables and hardly any chips. Even on birthdays.

However, Sparky couldn't say any of this to Grandad. As far as he knew, they were looking for ideas for a party for someone special like God, not Mr Smart – even though Mr Smart was special too.

Beryl had plenty of other suggestions, but the section that caught Sparky's eye had the title 'Activity birthdays'. Now *that* sounded more like it.

'Let's look at those, Grandad,' she said.

As her eyes scanned the screen, they began to glow with excitement. There was everything from horse-riding to snorkelling to bowling to...

Sparky sucked in a breath. Her hand shot out and she pointed. 'There, Grandad – there! It's perfect!'

Grandad leaned forward and followed Sparky's finger.

'Really?' he said. 'Are you sure? The special someone would have to be very brave. *Are* they very brave?'

'Oh, they are, Grandad! Ever so brave! It's the best idea in the whole world.'

* * * *

A little later, Grandad walked Sparky home. They arrived just as Mrs Smart drove into the driveway with Sissy after a hard day at school.

'You look cheerful, Sparky,' said Mrs Smart. 'What have you been up to?'

'Nothing really,' Sparky replied. 'In fact, nothing at all.' But the pink spot of excitement that bloomed on each cheek said otherwise.

Mrs Smart's eyes narrowed. 'Hmm,' she muttered. Then, 'Cup of tea, Dad?' she offered to Grandad.

Grandad shook his head. 'Very kind, but I must be off.'

Normally, Sparky would have tried to persuade Grandad to stay. She liked it when he stopped for tea. Not only did it mean she had longer to spend with him (he was, after all, her very best friend), it also meant she could put off doing her homework for at least another hour.

Today, however, Sparky didn't say a word. She was relieved that Grandad couldn't stop. All she wanted to do was tell Mrs Smart about Beryl's brilliant idea for

Mr Smart's birthday party. But she couldn't do it while Grandad was there because it was a secret.

'Mum, I've got something to tell you,' Sparky announced when the coast was clear.

Mrs Smart flicked on the kettle to make a cup of tea and turned to look at her. 'I knew there was something. I always know when there's something. Your face gives you away every time.'

Hmm... thought Sparky. *I must work on my face...*

'Oh, it's nothing bad,' she said. 'Actually it's really good. Really, really good. The thing is, Grandad and I asked Beryl –'

Just then, Sparky was interrupted by the sound of a key turning in the front door.

'Hello!' Mr Smart called as he stepped into the hall. Sparky's face fell.

'Why are *you* home?' she snapped. 'You're never home this early. Never.'

Mr Smart looked taken aback. 'And it's nice to see you too, Sparky.'

'But why are you here?' she demanded.

'Sparky!' said Mrs Smart. 'Don't speak to your dad like that – he does live here.' She glanced up at Mr Smart. 'But actually, why *are* you here?'

'Mr Spriggs didn't want to go for his run. He's got a cold.'

'Does that mean you're finished for the day?' asked Sparky. 'You're not going out again?'

Mr Smart shook his head. 'Not today, no. Sorry to disappoint you.'

'Oh.' Sparky blew out her cheeks. Now she'd have to wait until tomorrow to tell Mrs Smart. That's if she didn't burst in the meantime!

'What were you saying about Beryl, Sparky?' asked Mrs Smart.

'Nothing,' Sparky moaned. 'I wish Grandad had stayed for tea because now I'll have to go and do my homework.' And she left the room.

A few moments later, Mr Smart knocked on her bedroom door. 'Only me. Can I come in?'

'Yes,' Sparky grunted. 'But I have to get on with my homework.'

'Of course,' said Mr Smart, opening the door. 'Are you all right?'

'Yes,' Sparky grunted again.

'You don't look all right.'

'I know. My face gives me away every time.'

'I'm not going to argue with that,' said Mr Smart. The corners of his mouth turned up slightly as he tried to hide a smile. Then, he cleared his throat and put on his most serious voice: 'The thing is, Sparky, I need your help.'

Mr Smart turned and glanced along the landing, then he pushed the door closed.

Sparky frowned. 'What do you need *my* help for?'

'Because,' said Mr Smart, perching on the end of the bed, 'you are my bright little spark and I need a really good idea.'

Now Sparky's interest was piqued. Really good ideas were, after all, her speciality. She dropped onto the bed next to him. 'What kind of idea?'

'Well' – Mr Smart lowered his voice – 'you know it's your mum's and my wedding anniversary at the end of the month?'

Sparky's eyes grew a little wider. She did know but

she'd forgotten. Mr and Mrs Smart didn't usually make a big thing of their anniversary. It was on the same day as Mr Smart's birthday and Mrs Smart always said that his birthday should be the main event.

'Erm... yes,' she said.

'Well, this year we'll have been married for 15 years,' Mr Smart continued. 'Can you believe it?'

'Erm... no,' Sparky said. What Sparky found even harder to believe was that Mr and Mrs Smart had had a life before she arrived on the planet.

'So, because we've been married for 15 years, and that makes it kind of a special anniversary, I thought it would be nice to celebrate it properly.'

'Oh...' Somewhere inside herself, Sparky noticed a slight sinking feeling.

'And it's on a Saturday this year, so we can do something on the day.' Dad chattered on. 'Mum won't be working and I can make sure I'm free too. But what I need, Sparky, is a fantastic idea. Oh, and the best bit? I want it to be a surprise. I don't want Mum to know, so not a word. You've got to promise!'

Sparky's sinking feeling turned into a huge, heavy, crushing rock that smashed down into the pit of her stomach. She stared at Mr Smart, open-mouthed.

Mr Smart stared back. 'Well?' he said. 'What do you think?'

Sparky gulped. Both her parents seemed to have decided to organise surprise celebrations for each other on *the same day*. And she couldn't tell either of them because they'd made her promise not to! What on earth was she supposed to think?!

'The thing is, Dad...' Sparky began. *Oh, come on, brain! If ever I needed you to think quickly, it's now!* 'The thing is, Dad,' she went on, 'you never really bother about your wedding anniversary because it's on the same day as your birthday. So I think you should just go on not bothering about it. Especially as 15 isn't really that special, is it? I mean it's not like being married for 40 years, or 50. Or 100. It's just sort of – well – ordinary. And I don't think Mum would want to celebrate it.'

Sparky paused and rummaged about in her brain to find something to say next. Mr Smart looked more than a little taken aback.

'So – do you know what *I* think would be a good idea?' she said. 'I think you should wait and give Mum her surprise when you've been married for longer. A lot, lot longer.'

Mr Smart's face fell. 'Well, I never thought you'd be such a damp squib, Sparky. I thought you'd love the idea.' He stood up from Sparky's bed. 'Anyway, I don't want to wait. Being married to your mum for 15 years is special to me and I want to let her know.'

'Yes,' agreed Sparky, ideas at last beginning to flow, 'I know 15 years is special. But you know what Mum's like. She won't be expecting a fuss. She won't *want* a fuss. She'll be just as happy doing nothing for your anniversary like you always do. And the thing about Mum is,' she added – and surely this would make Mr Smart change his mind – 'she *hates* surprises.'

Mr Smart blinked. 'Does she?'

'Oh, yes,' said Sparky. 'Totally hates them. In fact, they're her most un-favourite thing.'

'Are they?'

Sparky watched as a hint of uncertainty crept into Mr Smart's eyes... as he lifted a hand to stroke his chin... then dropped his head to one side to consider what Sparky had said.

Yesss! she thought. *My quick-thinking saves the day again!*

Clearly she'd managed to kill the surprise anniversary idea stone dead.

Mrs Smart's voice sailed up the stairs. 'Sparky! Have you seen your dad?'

'Yes, Mum,' Sparky called back. 'He's in here with me.'

'Well, Stanley's just phoned and needs picking up. Can you ask Dad to go and fetch him?'

'Dad,' said Sparky, 'can you go and fetch Stanley, please?'

'On my way!' Mr Smart called to Mrs Smart.

Before he left the room, Mr Smart gave Sparky a long, hard look. 'You know, you might not think 15 years is much of a milestone, Sparky, but I do. And I think Mum does too. As for not liking surprises, you're wrong. Everyone likes surprises.'

'*You* don't,' said Sparky. 'Stanley said so.'

'Did he? Why?' Fortunately, Mr Smart didn't give Sparky the chance to answer. 'Anyway, I'm going to organise something for Mum because it's a special day. So, if you'd like to help by coming up with some suggestions, that would be much appreciated.'

The stone in Sparky's stomach crashed down further. Harder and heavier this time. And as it fell, a rush of panic pushed upwards.

'But... but...' she spluttered, '**...you can't!** I mean, supposing Mum's organising a surprise for you on the same day because it's *your birthday*?'

Sparky sucked in a gasp of air and froze. **Oh, no! What had she done?** She couldn't stop the words from tumbling out and now she'd ruined everything. She'd given up Mrs Smart's secret and she'd broken her promise not to say anything.

Mr Smart gazed at her for a moment more. Then his mouth stretched into a wide smile. 'Sparky, is that what you're worried about? That Mum will have arranged something for me too?'

Sparky said nothing. Her mouth was frozen like the rest of her.

'You funny girl!' said Mr Smart. 'Mum *never* arranges anything for my birthday. Ever! We always just make it up on the day – which is why this could be such fun. It's the perfect opportunity to organise a surprise, because she simply won't be expecting anything.' He moved to the door. 'Anyway, I must go and get Stanley. But, seriously, you don't need to worry,' and he chuckled. 'Mum planning a surprise for my birthday? Never in a month of Sundays!'

Mr Smart left the room and Sparky found herself in what can only be described as a 'quandary'. ('Quandary' is an excellent word, by the way. If you've never come across it before, it's pronounced 'kwon-dree' and it means that Sparky didn't know which way to turn. Find a way to use the word 'quandary' next time you're talking to one of your teachers and they'll think you're very clever.)

The day of Mr Smart's birthday and Mr and Mrs Smart's wedding anniversary was turning into a calamity of the worst kind. And there didn't seem to be anything Sparky could do to stop it.

How can you stop one thing happening so that the other thing isn't a complete catastrophe (another very good word) when you've been sworn to secrecy? When you can't tell the very people who need to know, to avoid the mishap happening in the first place?

When actually, you can't tell *anyone*?

Sparky stood up from her bed and paced up and down. She sat down again. Then stood up again. She dug the list of spellings she was supposed to learn for tomorrow's class test out of her bag. She plonked back onto her bed and tried to concentrate on them, but it was impossible. The words swam in front of her eyes and rearranged themselves into party invitations:

IT'S MR SMART'S FORTIETH BIRTHDAY.
Please come to his SURPRISE party –
and make sure you keep it a secret!
Love from Mrs Smart x

Mrs Smart and I have been married for 15 years!
Please help us celebrate.
(But it's a surprise, so shhh!)
Lots of love, Mr Smart

The harder Sparky tried to concentrate, the more impossible it was. Tomorrow's spelling test was not going to go well.

At last, she heard Mr Smart get home with Stanley.

'About time, too,' she muttered to herself. She nipped out of her bedroom to stand at the top of the stairs.

Stanley crouched down by the front door, untying the laces of his trainers. Mr Smart was nowhere in sight, but Sparky could hear him talking to Mrs Smart in the kitchen.

'Pssst!'

Sparky wasn't usually the sort of girl to hiss like that at her brother, but if ever a situation called for a good hiss, it was this one.

Stanley didn't appear to hear.

'Psssst!' Sparky made her hiss a little louder and longer.

Stanley glanced round, then up the stairs. 'Sparky, why are you hissing?'

Sparky didn't answer. She just flapped her hands silently at him in what she hoped was a 'come-here-really-quite-urgently' sort of gesture.

Stanley stopped messing with his shoe laces and flapped his own hands back. 'What's all this?'

Sparky rolled her eyes. 'Come here!' she mouthed. Her lips moved in an exaggerated way as she tried to make them form the words without actually letting any sound escape her mouth.

'What is wrong with you?' Stanley shook his head. 'I'm trying to undo my shoelaces.' He returned his fingers to his laces, only to find that one of them had got into a knot. 'Now look what you've made me do...' He sighed and tutted, bending lower to address the problem.

Sparky could still hear Mr and Mrs Smart chatting in the kitchen. Since getting his trainers off was clearly going to take Stanley any amount of time from now until next weekend, Sparky knew she had no choice. She couldn't wait. After all, talking to Stanley had never been more urgent. She'd just have to run downstairs and whisper the details of the whole disastrous affair into his ear – and hope that Mr and Mrs Smart stayed in the kitchen and wouldn't notice a thing.

At the foot of the stairs, Sparky stopped. She couldn't see into the kitchen but could hear Mrs Smart begin to laugh. Then Mr Smart laughed too. Hopefully this meant they were having a cheerful conversation that would last at least another five minutes.

Sparky crept towards Stanley, who was still doing battle with the knotted lace. He was so intent on untying the lace that he didn't realise she was there.

Unfortunately for Sparky, *she* was so intent on giving Stanley the bad news that she didn't notice Sissy, who had just toddled out of the kitchen. As Sparky leant towards Stanley to whisper in his ear, Sissy spotted her and ran towards her.

If Sissy hadn't been hugging her pink unicorn, her cuddly rabbit called Richard, and a large board book about different things you can eat for breakfast, all might have been well. She might have noticed the one trainer Stanley had managed to take off, lying in the middle of the hall, before she reached it.

As it was... she didn't. The moment Sparky leant towards Stanley, Sissy (trotting at full-tilt) tripped over the trainer. While her toys and the breakfast board book went flying in all directions, Sissy herself flew head first into her older sister – who similarly flew head first into her older brother, knocking him and his knotted shoelace flat.

'Oi!' yelled Stanley to Sparky.

'Oi!' yelled Sparky to Sissy.

'Oi!' yelled Sissy to no one in particular. 'Oi, oi, oi!'

'What's going on?' yelled Mrs Smart, who appeared instantly from the kitchen.

Mr Smart followed. He didn't yell, although as it turned out, it might have been better if he had.

Stanley pulled himself back up to his crouching position. 'Don't ask me,' he said. 'Ask Sparky!'

He lost his balance and sat down again hard – on something rather soft.

Sissy stuck out her bottom lip. 'Aww!' she cried and stretched out her arms. 'Poor Wichard!'

Mrs Smart raised her hands and pressed them to her head for a moment. 'Sometimes,' she said in a quiet voice, 'this family is enough to give a headache to someone who *never* gets headaches.'

With that, she turned to flounce back into the kitchen.

What she didn't realise was that Mr Smart was standing right behind her. (Which is why it would have been better if he'd yelled. Had he yelled, she would have known exactly where he was.) As Mrs Smart turned, she smacked hard into him. Most of the coffee in the mug in his hand shot up into the air and slopped straight down again – onto Mrs Smart's head. Of course, it didn't

stay on her head. When liquid falls onto something with nothing to hold it, it runs away – you can check it in a science book. So Mr Smart's coffee ran, trickled and dripped all the way down Mrs Smart to her feet.

Silence. Nobody moved. Nobody even breathed.

After what seemed like an age, Mrs Smart inhaled deeply. All she could smell was coffee, as she pushed back her coffee-soaked hair.

'I'm so sorry, Stell –' Mr Smart began, only to be instantly shushed as Mrs Smart held a hand up for silence.

She turned and began to walk, in the odd sort of way you walk when you're quite wet, towards the stairs. As she passed close to Sparky, Sissy and Stanley, Sparky opened her mouth to speak.

'Not a word,' murmured Mrs Smart. 'From any of you. Not. A. Word.'

Sissy giggled. 'Not. A. Nerd,' she said.

When it was time to get up for school the next morning, Sparky groaned. She'd hardly slept all night. A disaster to end all disasters was about to happen in her family and she hadn't been able to talk about it to anyone.

She couldn't talk about it with Mr and Mrs Smart, for obvious reasons. Stanley had refused to open his bedroom door when she'd tried to speak to him later in the evening. And although Sissy might have been quite happy to hear all the ins and outs of the surprises that were about to go terribly wrong, she probably wouldn't have had anything useful to add.

This was one occasion when Sparky hadn't even talked to God. *There's no point telling Him,* she thought. *He already knows. Anyway, it's not up to God to sort this out, it's up to me. And I don't know how.*

'You're not your usual chatty self,' said Grandad Bagg, as he and Sparky walked to school. 'And that's a very serious face you're wearing too.'

Sparky sighed. There her face went, giving her away again. 'That's because I feel serious, Grandad. You'd feel serious too if you had to solve a problem that no one in the whole world could possibly solve.'

Grandad's heavy eyebrows stumbled into each other. 'No one?' he said. 'Absolutely no one? Not even me?'

Sparky raised her serious eyes to look at him. 'Not even you, Grandad,' she said, and shook her head sadly.

They walked on in silence.

'What about God?' Grandad asked. 'Have you asked God?'

Sparky shook her head again. 'He already knows. Anyway, this is the one thing He wouldn't be able to do anything about. It's a **Monstrous Mishap of Megatastic Proportions** – and it hasn't even happened yet.'

Grandad was so surprised, he stopped walking. 'Do you know, Sparky, I don't think I've ever heard you use so many big words before.'

Sparky stopped walking too. 'That's because I've never had such a gigantic problem before.'

Grandad put his hand on Sparky's shoulder. He smiled, and the twinkle that was always in his eyes twinkled more kindly than ever. 'A problem shared is a problem halved, you know.'

'But that's just it, Grandad,' Sparky replied. 'I *can't* share it. If I do, I'll spoil the surprise.'

'I see,' said Grandad, and he rubbed an ear in a thoughtful sort of way. 'A surprise, you say? This wouldn't have anything to do with the surprise birthday party we asked Beryl about yesterday, would it? The one for someone special, like God – although not God, obviously?'

'No!' said Sparky, far too quickly. 'I mean, there are all sorts of surprises. They don't always have to be for parties. Or birthdays. A surprise can be for anything... I'm always surprised when I get a wobbly tooth,' she added. 'Aren't you?'

'Not so much,' Grandad replied. 'At my age I'm just grateful for the teeth that *don't* wobble.'

At the school gate, Sparky cuddled into Grandad's squidgy tummy and said goodbye.

'Bye for now, Sparky,' said Grandad. 'See you at the end of the day. And by the way, there's nothing God can't do. If you've got a problem, you tell Him all about it. He'll find a way to sort it out, I promise. But you've got to talk to Him.'

Sparky waved and went to the cloakroom to hang up her coat. But instead of then heading to her classroom, she went to the girls' toilets, slipped into a cubicle and locked the door. She did the same thing at morning break,

and after lunch. If anyone had seen her, they'd probably have thought she had a funny tummy.

She didn't. Inside the cubicle, Sparky talked to God – very quietly so as not to draw attention to herself. If someone called out, 'Is anyone in that toilet?' she didn't answer. Not even when it was her friend, Madeleine.

'Is anyone in that toilet?' Madeleine called.

Sparky did worry that, if she didn't answer, Madeleine might get down on the floor and peer under the door to try to see if her cubicle was empty. Madeleine did things like that. But luckily, this didn't seem to be a day when Madeleine was in the mood for peering under doors, and she disappeared again quite quickly.

So Sparky was left in peace to have a good, long talk

with God about the Monstrous Mishap of Megatastic Proportions – even though she knew He knew all about it already.

At two o'clock in the afternoon, Sparky sat down to do the class spelling test. It went very badly indeed.

At half past two, Sparky spoke to God again (in her head) as she sat at her desk.

At three o'clock in the afternoon, Sparky had an idea while her teacher, Mr Barber, was talking about pollen. (If you're anything like Sparky, you're probably wondering why a teacher would be called Mr Barber. It would make far more sense for a barber to be called Mr Barber and a teacher to be called Mr Teacher.) Why Mr Barber was talking about pollen, Sparky had no idea. She wasn't listening. In fact, she had barely listened to a word Mr Barber had said all day.

The only person Sparky wanted to listen to was God. And she was pretty sure that God had spoken to her at three o'clock. Sparky may be the Quick-thinking Queen of Bright Ideas, but when it came to sorting out Monstrous Mishaps of Megatastic Proportions, she was learning that God was the King of Awesome Answers.

☆ ☆ ☆ ☆

'Grandad!' Sparky flung herself into Grandad Bagg's squidgy tummy when she spotted him at the school gate at home time.

'**Oof!**' gasped Grandad. 'Steady on! Well, I must say, you look much more cheerful than you did this morning.'

Sparky beamed. 'That's because I am!'

'Sounds like a good day, then,' said Grandad. 'How did

your spelling test go?'

'Terribly! Really, *really* badly!' Sparky's eyes sparkled.

'Oh,' said Grandad, a little confused. 'And what's Mr Barber been teaching you?'

'I haven't a clue,' answered Sparky. 'I haven't been listening all day long!' She grinned.

'Hmm,' said Grandad. 'I'm not sure that's something you should be looking quite so happy about.'

'Oh, it's not *that* that's making me happy,' Sparky replied. 'It's what *you* said.'

'Is it?' Grandad looked mystified.

'Grandad, don't tell me you've forgotten already?'

'Of course not. I never forget things. I just file them away somewhere in my brain cabinet and can't see them anymore.'

Sparky laughed. '**You told me to talk to God and I did!**'

'Ah!' said Grandad. 'And He solved your Monstrous Mishap of Megatastic Proportions, did He?'

'Yes!' Sparky shrieked. 'It's brilliant! Far too brilliant an idea for me to have come up with all by myself.'

'God's nothing if not brilliant,' agreed Grandad.

'I mean, I haven't talked to the person I need to talk to yet,' Sparky added. 'But I think they'll be fine with it.'

'Well, I certainly hope so. Now, I need to pop home and do a spot of work in the greenhouse.'

'Singing to your tomatoes?' asked Sparky.

'Yes, that too. How would you fancy joining me in a little duet?'

* * * *

'Mum?' said Sparky when she finally got home at the end of the day. 'What time will Dad be back?'

'I'm not sure,' said Mrs Smart. She was in the bathroom trying to rinse honey out of Sissy's hair. A lot of honey in a lot of hair. 'Half an hour... An hour...'

Sparky made a face. 'An *hour*? But that's ages! I want him to be home now.'

Mrs Smart glanced at her. 'Yesterday you were annoyed when Dad got home early. Today you can't wait for him to get back. I wish I understood what went on in that head of yours. You're a funny one, Sparky Smart.'

'Parky Mart... Parky Mart,' sang Sissy.

Mrs Smart reached for a towel to dry Sissy's hair.

'Helloo!' a voice called. 'Anyone home?'

'Dad!'

Sparky shot out of the bathroom and down the stairs. She would have flung herself into Mr Smart's tummy the way she'd done with Grandad's – if Mr Smart hadn't been quite so sweaty and stinky from work.

'Dad,' hissed Sparky. 'We need to talk.'

'Do we?' Mr Smart was a little taken aback. 'What about?'

Sparky shook her head. 'Not here.' She glanced up towards the bathroom. 'When Mum comes down with Sissy, say you're going upstairs for a quick shower. Then meet me in my bedroom.'

'Right,' said Mr Smart. 'Because...?'

'Oh, *you* know!' hissed Sparky, and she gave him a big wink.

Whether or not Mr Smart actually did know what Sparky was talking about, he decided to follow her instructions. When Mrs Smart went down to the kitchen with Sissy, Mr Smart said he was going to have a quick shower, and went up to Sparky's room.

'Now it won't be long till Mum discovers you're in here instead of in the shower,' Sparky said. 'So I need you to be really quiet and listen. The thing is, I was wrong about your fifteenth wedding anniversary. It isn't ordinary at all. It's amazing and fantastic. And you have to put up with a *lot* from Sissy and Stanley. And quite a lot from me too... sometimes. So I think you should definitely celebrate, and do it as a surprise. That'll be really nice for Mum. But I think you should definitely *not* do it on your birthday.'

'But my birthday *is* our wedding anniversary, Sparky,' said Mr Smart.

'I know!' said Sparky. 'And as it's your birthday and it's a Saturday, then we're bound to all do something together to say happy birthday to you, like we always do. It might not be organised,' she added quickly, 'but it'll still be something. And Mum will be sad if we don't do that. So' – and this was Sparky's big idea – 'you should arrange your anniversary surprise *for the day after.* That way, Mum will be expecting it even less, and you'll be able to have a whole weekend of celebrations instead of just one measly day.'

Sparky's words had spilled out in such a rush that when she'd finished, she was almost out of breath.

Mr Smart looked at her for a moment, then sat down on the end of the bed.

Sparky was on tenterhooks. 'Well?'

'Do you know what, Sparky?' said Mr Smart. 'That's actually not such a daft idea.'

'Really?' Sparky's grin grew so wide, it simply couldn't

stretch any further.

'Really,' answered Mr Smart with a nod. Then his eyes narrowed the tiniest bit. 'I tell you what, though,' he added, 'if I didn't know better, I'd say there was something going on.'

Sparky shook her head. 'Nothing going on here, Dad,' she said. 'Nothing at all. And, Dad?'

'Yes, Sparky?'

'Can you get off my bed now, please? You stink.'

As Mr Smart went to have his shower, Sparky skipped downstairs.

In the kitchen, Sissy's mouth and hands were full of more bread and honey, while Mrs Smart sipped a cup of tea.

'By the way, Sparky,' said Mrs Smart, 'what was it you and Grandad asked Beryl yesterday? You never did tell me.'

Sparky threw a furtive glance towards the stairs and pushed the kitchen door closed. 'Well, I didn't tell Grandad about Dad's surprise party. But I *did* ask him what he thought would make a good surprise party idea. So we asked Beryl, and she found the perfect thing.'

'Oh, really? Then let's hear it, because so far I haven't come up with anything.'

Sparky began to jiggle with excitement. 'All right then, it's... skydiving!'

Mrs Smart sat with her mug of tea midway to her mouth. 'Skydiving?' she repeated.

'Yes!' said Sparky. 'Isn't Beryl brilliant?'

'Skydiving,' Mrs Smart said again.

'Yes!'

'As in going up in an aeroplane and then throwing yourself out of it?'

'Yes! I mean, with a parachute – obviously.'

Mrs Smart put her mug down on the table. She tried to picture Mr Smart's face when she told him that she'd arranged for him to jump out of an aeroplane as a birthday treat.

Mr Smart, who hated aeroplanes and so had never flown anywhere.

Mr Smart, who hid it well, but was actually terrified of heights.

And she began to giggle.

'Well?' said Sparky. 'Wouldn't that be just the best surprise ever?'

'Oh, yes,' spluttered Mrs Smart. 'And if not the best, then certainly the biggest.'

Once more, Sparky's face wore the widest grin she could fit onto it. 'So, is that a yes?'

'Let me see,' replied Mrs Smart, as she tried to stifle her chuckles. 'How can I put this, Sparky? Erm... no. It's most *definitely* a no.'

☆ ☆ ☆ ☆

Sparky opened her eyes. Still in bed, she stretched and yawned. She could see a glimmer of daylight through a crack in the curtains, so it must be morning.

With a kick of her legs, she flicked back her duvet and lifted her head to glance towards Sissy. Sissy still seemed to be fast asleep.

Sparky smiled. It was Saturday. Sparky loved Saturdays. She gave her toes a happy wriggle and let her eyes drift shut again.

They stayed shut for about four seconds. On the fifth

second, they sprang wide open.

Sparky had suddenly remembered: this wasn't just any old Saturday. This was a special Saturday. A super-duper Saturday.

A stupendously sparkling Saturday!

This was the Saturday of Mr Smart's fortieth birthday and Mr and Mrs Smart's fifteenth wedding anniversary.

The *best* weekend of the year!

Sparky sprang out of bed. Even the sound of her springing didn't disturb Sissy, who slept soundly on.

Of course, Mr and Mrs Smart wouldn't still be asleep. *How could they be?* Sparky thought, as she skipped along the landing. *It would be impossible for anyone to still be asleep with such an exciting day ahead of them,* she said to herself, as she burst into Mr and Mrs Smart's bedroom. *No one would even* want *to be asleep on a day as exciting as this one!* she decided, as she jumped onto the end of Mr and Mrs Smart's bed and jiggled up and down.

Sparky wasn't always right, however. Mr and Mrs Smart *were* still asleep. And they were quite happy to be asleep. They would probably have stayed asleep too, had it not been for Sparky's enthusiastic bouncing.

Mrs Smart opened one bleary eye. 'Sparky...' She forced open the other eye. 'Sparky, what's going on? What are you doing?'

'What am *I* doing?' Sparky's jaw dropped. 'What are *you* doing? This is the weekend of Dad's birthday and your wedding anniversary. How can you possibly *still be asleep*?'

'Well,' grunted Mr Smart, 'we're certainly not asleep now.'

'But *no one* stays asleep on the morning of their birthday and wedding anniversary!' Sparky insisted.

'Absolutely, positively *no one*!'

'No one with a nearly-nine-year-old bouncing on their bed, anyway,' murmured Mrs Smart and closed her eyes once more. 'I tell you what, though...' She turned towards Mr Smart, still with her eyes closed. 'Happy birthday, sweetheart.'

Mr Smart smiled. His eyes were closed as well. 'And a very happy wedding anniversary,' he said.

'Oh, yes,' replied Mrs Smart. 'That too.'

Sparky's jaw dropped a little wider. As special, super-duper, stupendously sparkling Saturdays went, this one was more like a wet bag of flour.

Then, all of a sudden, Mr Smart's eyes flicked open. '**Oh, no**,' he said.

'What?' mumbled Mrs Smart.

'You haven't... have you?' said Mr Smart.

'Haven't what?' answered Mrs Smart.

'*You* know.'

'No, I don't know.'

'You haven't...' Mr Smart began again. 'You haven't... organised anything. Have you?'

Mrs Smart's still bleary eyes opened too. 'Anything – like what?'

'Like... a surprise party. I mean, it is my fortieth birthday, and surprise parties are sort of a thing when you get to that age. You wouldn't have done anything like that – would you?'

'Oh...' Mrs Smart looked anxious. 'You see, I was going to, I really was. I really, *really* was.'

'Were you?' Mr Smart looked anxious too.

'She was,' replied Sparky.

'Only then I was so busy with school. And Sissy – well, she has been quite a handful lately. And there's been so much to do here. And I thought and thought and *thought* – I really did. But in the end... I just couldn't think of any sort of surprise you'd actually want.'

'She couldn't,' said Sparky.

Mr Smart looked less anxious. 'That's good,' he said. 'Because I was planning to surprise you for our wedding anniversary. Because it's our fifteenth and it's special. Only, I couldn't come up with a surprise you might enjoy either.'

Mrs Smart looked less anxious too. 'Really?'

Mr Smart nodded. 'Really.'

'So, for your birthday and for our wedding anniversary, we can just do what we normally do?'

'I hope so,' replied Mr Smart. 'Make it up as we go along.'

Mrs Smart smiled. 'Sounds good to me.'

Mr Smart beamed. 'Sounds *terrific* to me!'

'Me too,' said Sparky.

'And when you think about it,' Mr Smart added, 'because we make it up as we go along, *all* my birthdays and our anniversaries end up being surprises. The best surprises ever.'

STORY 2

The wrong toilet

'For some families,' said Sparky, 'a new pair of glasses would be *exactly* that – just a new pair of glasses. And nothing else. Which is actually quite boring.'

Mr Smart said nothing. He simply folded his arms and watched the police car drive away. The crowd that had gathered had mostly sloped off by now. There was just a handful of people left, who stared and whispered and nudged each other.

'But for *our* family,' Sparky continued, 'getting a new pair of glasses has turned into probably the biggest adventure we'll have all year.'

Mr Smart's eyes flicked towards her. 'You say that as if it's a good thing,' he muttered.

'I'm sure it *is* a good thing,' Sparky replied.

'Well, I'm so glad you think so, Sparky,' huffed Mr Smart. 'That makes me feel *loads* better.'

Stanley looked miserable. 'It doesn't make *me* feel better,' he grunted. 'This has been the worst day of my life.'

'Yes,' agreed Mr Smart. 'Possibly mine too. And we haven't even told your mum about it yet.'

'Do we *have* to tell her?' Stanley's face sank further into its miserable expression.

'Of course we have to tell her. And if *we* don't, someone else is bound to.'

'They might not,' chirped Sparky. 'Although, if they don't, I suppose she'll probably just see it in the newspaper.'

Mr Smart sighed and raised his eyes.

Stanley dropped his head into his hands. 'Why?' he moaned. 'Why, oh why – of all the families I could have been born into – did I have to be born a Smart...?'

Two weeks earlier, Mr and Mrs Smart had sat with Stanley on a bench outside his classroom. It was parents' evening at Stanley's school. Grandad Bagg was away on a little break to Cornwall and, as he wasn't able to childmind (which, to be fair, he did rather a lot), Sparky and Sissy sat there too – Sparky next to them on the bench, Sissy on the floor.

The evening was almost over. They'd seen all Stanley's other teachers. Now they just had to wait to speak to his class tutor.

'Sissy, don't sit on the floor,' Mrs Smart said. 'It's probably very dirty. Hundreds of feet walk on this lino, you know.'

Sissy didn't move.

'Come on, Sissy,' said Mr Smart. 'Come and sit on my lap.'

'Nap, nap, nap,' said Sissy. And she stayed where she was.

'Sit next to me, Sissy,' invited Sparky. 'It's nicer up here on the bench.'

Sissy picked up a small piece of dry mud. At least, it looked like dry mud – the sort of clumpy dry mud that might have fallen off a football boot. She held it out to Mrs Smart.

'Mub, Mummy,' she said.

Stanley wrinkled his nose. 'Sissy, that's disgusting.'

Mr Smart was about to reach down to lift Sissy onto his lap when the classroom door swung open.

'Sorry to keep you waiting,' said Mrs Goodbook-Jolly, Stanley's tutor. 'Do come in.'

Stanley had often remarked to Mr and Mrs Smart that

it would make far more sense for Mrs Goodbook-Jolly to be called Mrs Jolly-Goodbook. No doubt you'll agree with him.

Mr Smart pulled Sissy up off the floor. No sooner was she in his arms than she waved the small piece of (probably) mud in the air – and accidentally (and rather unfortunately) stuck it up his nose.

Mr Smart let out a strange cry: **'Urr-argh!'**

Mrs Smart, Mrs Goodbook-Jolly, Stanley and Sparky turned to stare at him.

'Mubby nosey, Daddy,' Sissy giggled.

Mr Smart held his daughter out towards Mrs Smart. 'Could you howed Sissy for a bowbent?' He sounded as though he had a dreadful cold. 'I'll be back in a binute.' And he disappeared to the nearest toilets to fetch some tissue.

'Shall we carry on?' asked Mrs Goodbook-Jolly.

'Yes,' replied Mrs Smart. 'Probably best.'

They sat down and Mrs Goodbook-Jolly told them all how well Stanley was getting on at school; how polite he was; how he worked hard and was always on time with his homework and how pleased all his teachers were to have him in their classes.

Mrs Smart glowed with pride. Stanley went pink with embarrassment.

'There is one thing, however,' said Mrs Goodbook-Jolly.

Mrs Smart stopped glowing and frowned. 'Is there?'

'Oh, it's nothing terrible,' said Mrs Goodbook-Jolly. 'It's just that I and some of Stanley's other teachers wonder if he might need glasses.'

Mrs Smart and Sparky glanced at Stanley.

Sissy glanced up towards the shelf beside her. A very real-looking plastic skull sat on it. Stanley tried not to glance anywhere or at anyone.

'Well...' said Mrs Smart. 'I mean, I don't think he does. I'd be very surprised. No one wears glasses in our family. No one. Not even Grandad, and he's 71.'

'It's just that,' Mrs Goodbook-Jolly continued, 'Stanley does seem to struggle a bit when something's written on the whiteboard. If he has to copy anything down, sometimes he waits until the end of the class and then goes and stands at the front to see better.'

'Does he?' Mrs Smart looked shocked. She turned to Stanley. 'Do you?'

Stanley shrugged his shoulders. 'Not really... Well, only sometimes. And it's mostly when I'm sitting behind someone with a really big head.'

Mrs Goodbook-Jolly raised an eyebrow. 'I wasn't aware that we had any pupils with really big heads.'

'Well, some of them seem quite big when you're sitting behind them,' said Stanley.

Mr Smart reappeared. 'What have I missed?' he asked, and he dabbed at his nose with a tissue.

'Mrs Goodbook-Jolly thinks Stanley needs glasses,' said Mrs Smart. '*I* don't think he does, do you? I'll be very surprised. I mean, no one in our family wears glasses. No one. Not even Grandad, and he's 71.'

'Stanley?' asked Sparky. 'Is that why you sometimes sit on the floor right in front of the TV instead of on your special bit of the sofa?'

'I don't,' said Stanley. His pinkness from embarrassment turned to a deeper redness from awkwardness. 'When have you ever seen me sit on the floor to watch TV?'

'Lots of times. Well, a few anyway. When you think no one's looking.'

'Are you having trouble seeing the TV, Stanley?' asked Mr Smart.

'No.' Stanley shook his head. 'Just the weather forecast sometimes. The place names on the map.'

'Right,' said Mr Smart.

'Right,' said Mrs Smart.

There was silence.

'I do think it might be worth just having a check with an optician,' said Mrs Goodbook-Jolly. 'Don't you?'

Mrs Smart sighed. 'I mean, yes, I suppose so. If Stanley needs glasses, then he needs glasses. I'll just be very surprised, that's all, because no one in our family wears glasses. No one. Not even Grandad, and he's...'

'...71. Yes, I understand,' said Mrs Goodbook-Jolly. 'It won't hurt to check, though, will it? Then you'll know for sure.'

* * * *

'I don't know what the problem is,' said Sparky. '**I like them**.'

Stanley (who had been to the optician and, as it turned out, did need glasses) shot her a moody glance. The new glasses lay folded up on the table in front of him.

'You only like them,' he grumbled, 'because you don't have to wear them.'

Sparky shrugged her shoulders. 'I'll wear them, if you like. Pass them over.'

'I'm not letting you wear my glasses, Sparky,' Stanley

snapped. 'You don't need glasses for a start. *Your* eyes work.'

'Your eyes work a bit. You don't have to wear glasses the whole time.'

'I don't want to wear them at all!'

Mrs Smart held up her hands. 'All right, can we just leave it now, please? We seem to have talked about nothing but glasses since parents' evening. Now, I'm sorry you need glasses, Stanley, but that seems to be the way it is. So you'll just have to try to get used to them.'

'I don't want to get used to them.'

'Well,' said Sparky, 'if you didn't spend so much time peering at weather stuff on the computer, maybe you wouldn't even need them.'

Stanley's jaw dropped. 'Weather *stuff*? The weather is actually very important – much more important than those stupid cartoons you watch. And do you know what I really don't get?'

'No, Stanley, what do you really not get?'

'What I don't get is why God allows *your* eyes to work perfectly when all you do is watch stupid cartoons on the TV, but He's let *mine* go wrong even though when I use the computer it's for something important!'

'Oh, Stanley!' Mrs Smart reached out to take Stanley's hand as it rested on the table next to his glasses. 'Stanley, God hasn't done this.'

Stanley snatched his hand away. 'Well, if God hasn't, then who has?'

'I told you,' said Sparky. 'You've done it yourself by spending too much time staring at weather stuff on the computer!'

'Sabrina!' Mrs Smart's eye was perilously close to a twitch. She took in a deep breath to calm herself down. 'Stanley, sometimes these things just happen. Sometimes our bodies don't work quite the way we want them to. It's not something God does. But what God *has* done is give people clever brains so that they can learn to be doctors and dentists – and opticians. Then we can go and see those people for help when we need to.'

The sound of a key in the front door meant that Mr Smart was home. He'd popped out for an evening run with Mr Obi next door.

'Thank goodness for that,' said Mrs Smart. 'Now Dad can deal with the glasses crisis for a bit and I can go and get some jobs done.'

She stood up from the table and went to march out to the hall. Before she'd even reached the kitchen door, however, she was met by Mr Smart and Mr Obi.

'Oh,' she said. 'Hello.'

'Hello, Stella,' said Mr Obi. 'I gather you've got a bit of a glasses crisis going on, so I thought it might help if I came and had a word.'

Mr Obi wore glasses. Very sleek, smart glasses. Mr Obi worked with computers and Mr Smart was always saying how clever he was. Mr Obi's glasses made him look even cleverer.

Mr Smart stood behind Mr Obi and winked at Mrs Smart.

'Well,' said Mrs Smart, 'that's very kind of you. That's very kind of Mr Obi, isn't it, Stanley?' She looked over towards him.

Stanley said nothing.

'I think it's a jolly good idea,' she added. 'After all, none of us can really talk to you about wearing glasses because we don't know what it's like.' She turned back to Mr Obi. 'You see, no one else in this family wears glasses. No one. Not even Grandad, and he's 71...'

The rest of the Smarts left the room, leaving Stanley and Mr Obi to have a heart to heart about the good things, and the not-so-good things, of wearing glasses. And when Mr Obi left an hour later, Stanley was a changed Smart.

His glasses were no longer folded up on the table. They were on his face. And Stanley didn't look uncomfortable or awkward or as though he would rather have *anything* on his face but a pair of glasses – oh, no. He looked proud to be wearing them. Truly proud. Not only that, but somehow he seemed more grown up.

Wow! thought Sparky. *Mr Obi is actually a glasses-wearing genius!*

'I don't know what it is, Stanley,' said Mrs Smart, 'but your glasses honestly do make you look more grown up.'

'More clever, I reckon,' added Sparky. 'Which is good because you needed a bit of help with that.'

'Yes, definitely more intelligent,' agreed Mr Smart. 'More –'

'More like a TV weather person?' said Stanley.

Mr Smart nodded. 'Well... yes.'

'That's what Mr Obi said. I said I didn't want to be the sort of TV weather person who had to wear glasses. But Mr Obi said if he had to choose between a TV weather person with glasses and one without, he'd pick the one with glasses every time. He said he reckoned wearing glasses would help me to develop... what was it...? *A strong TV weather persona.*'

'Did he indeed?' Mr Smart looked impressed. 'Well, if Mr Obi says it, it must be so. He's the cleverest person I know.'

Mrs Smart's face had taken on a wistful sort of expression.

'What's the matter, Mum?' asked Sparky. 'You do think Stanley looks good in his glasses, don't you?'

'Yes, of course,' Mrs Smart replied. 'It's just that they do make you look all grown up, Stanley. And I remember when you were just my little baby.'

Behind his glasses, Stanley rolled his eyes and tried to

change the subject. 'By the way, that film Sparky and I want to go to is still on at the cinema this weekend. Can we go, please?'

'Ooh, yes, can we?' said Sparky. 'And now Stanley's got his glasses, he might even be able to see it.'

'Oh...' Mrs Smart rested her hands on her hips. 'It's just that I've got a few things to do this weekend. I'm actually quite busy.' She glanced at Mr Smart.

He shook his head. 'Sorry, can't help. I've got a couple of extra training sessions booked in and a pile of paperwork to sort out.'

Stanley was about to make a fuss when Mr Smart had an idea. 'Wait a minute, though. Why don't you and Sparky go on your own?'

Mrs Smart's mouth dropped open for a few seconds before she spoke. 'Pardon?'

'**Really?**' Sparky's mouth was open too. 'You'd let us go to the cinema without you? Completely by ourselves and everything?'

'Yup,' said Mr Smart.

'Well, I'm not sure about that,' said Mrs Smart.

'Why not?' replied Stanley. 'I think it's a cool idea.'

Sparky beamed. 'Me too!'

'So do I,' said Mr Smart. 'They'll be fine, the two of them together. You said it yourself – Stanley does look very grown up.'

Mrs Smart gave Mr Smart a long, hard stare. 'Yes... *darling*... but there's a world of difference between *looking* grown up and actually *being* grown up... isn't there?'

Mr Smart nodded. 'True. But Stanley is 13 now. He's more than able to look out for Sparky at the cinema.'

Sparky made a face. 'I don't need looking out for.'

'One of us can drop them off and pick them up,' Mr Smart added. 'Can't see there being a problem.'

With her eyes still fixed on Mr Smart, Mrs Smart lifted her hands and pushed her hair back. 'Yes, well, let's see, shall we?'

'But...' began Mr Smart.

'After all,' Mrs Smart ploughed on, 'we don't need to make a decision right this very minute – *do we?*'

Stanley and Sparky glanced from one parent to the other.

'Fine,' said Stanley. 'I'll be in my room doing my homework.' And he stomped off.

'Fine,' said Sparky. 'I'll be in Stanley's room too.'

Stanley stopped halfway up the stairs and turned. 'Why?'

'Because at times like this, you and me, we need to stick together, Stanley,' Sparky replied, and trotted up the stairs behind him.

Stanley and Sparky stood on the pavement outside the cinema. Mrs Smart and Mr Smart (who held on tight to Sissy's hand) stood with them. Lately, if you didn't want Sissy to escape, you had to hold on to her hand tightly. She had developed what Sparky called the 'tuggle-twisty'. When someone held her hand, if she tugged it at just the right moment and followed the tug with a quick twist, she could free herself in a matter of seconds.

Sparky thought it was ingenious.

Mrs Smart had taken it as another sign that her babies

were all growing up far too quickly.

'Now, you're sure you don't want us to come in with you and help you buy the tickets?' asked Mrs Smart. A strand of hair had fallen across one eye. It made her look even more anxious.

'No, thanks, Mum,' said Stanley. 'We do know how to buy tickets. We'll be fine.'

'We'll be fine,' Sparky repeated.

'Why don't we come in anyway – just to make sure?' said Mrs Smart.

'They'll be fine,' said Mr Smart. 'Besides, I think someone's keen to get going.'

Having discovered that a tuggle-twisty was having no effect on Mr Smart's firm grip, Sissy had now begun to pull. And pull and pull.

And whine: 'Gooo naaaaoww!'

'Bye, Mum,' said Sparky. 'Bye, Dad.'

'Yeah, bye,' said Stanley.

Mr Smart waved with his free hand. 'Have fun.'

'One of us will be back here at six o'clock,' added Mrs Smart. 'Six o'clock – you've got that, haven't you? We'll be waiting for you right here,' and she pointed at the pavement. 'Right here! And remember, Stanley, you're in charge!'

Sparky and Stanley were already at the cinema's main entrance. They waved to Mr and Mrs Smart as the wide glass doors slid back. The next moment, the pair of them had slipped inside.

Sparky's grin stretched across her whole face. 'Stanley, this is so exciting! We're at the cinema – on our own!'

Stanley shrugged his shoulders. He looked quite cool

and calm about the whole business. 'So?' he replied. 'It's just being a grown-up.'

Tickets bought, the two 'grown-up' Smarts made their way to the right studio and, after a bit of peering and pointing, found their seats. They were on the end of a row.

'I like being on the end,' said Sparky.

'Why?' asked Stanley.

'It makes it easier to get out to the toilet.'

'Why don't you go to the toilet now? If you go while the film's on, you'll miss it.' Stanley felt even more grown up as he issued advice.

'Because I don't *need* to go to the toilet now,' replied Sparky. 'But if I *do* need to go later, I'll be able to get out really easily. You're the only one I'll have to climb over.'

Stanley opened the bag of sweets he'd just bought and offered one to his sister.

'Shouldn't we wait till the film starts?' Sparky asked.

'Why?'

'Mum always makes us wait for sweets until the film starts.'

'Yes, but Mum's not here, is she?' Stanley adjusted his glasses. 'I'm in charge.'

Sparky had to agree that Stanley's glasses had indeed turned him into an in-charge sort of Smart. Perhaps, she thought, this *was* God's idea all along. So she took a sweet and popped it into her mouth.

Five minutes later, the lights dimmed and the film started. (Well, not the film itself. First, there were quite a few advertisements and bits of films that weren't out yet. You know the sort of thing – you've probably been to the cinema lots of times.)

By the time the film *actually* started, Stanley's bag of sweets was empty.

About a quarter of an hour later, Stanley leaned towards Sparky and whispered, 'I just need the toilet.'

Sparky put her hands on her hips – as much as you can when you're sitting in a cinema seat. 'You told *me* to go before the film started. Otherwise I'd miss it.'

'But I didn't need to go before it started.'

'Exactly!' hissed Sparky. 'And neither did I.'

'I'll be back in a minute. Stay here and don't move.'

'Of course I'm not going to move.' Stanley's glasses may have made him look more intelligent but Sparky was beginning to think it was just that – a look, and no more.

'If I move, I'll miss the film – just like you're going to.'

As Stanley slipped out of his seat and disappeared into the dark aisle, Sparky returned to watching the film. She was only vaguely aware of the doors to the studio being opened and then swinging closed again.

A short while later, the same doors swung open and closed again, and Stanley returned to his seat.

He leaned towards Sparky and whispered, 'What have I missed?'

'Well...' But that's as far as Sparky got. As she glanced at him, two things happened.

First, Sparky was aware that Stanley looked different from the way he'd looked before he went to the toilet.

Second, Sparky realised why. She raised a hand and pointed at his face. **'Stanley! Where are your glasses?'**

Stanley's hands flew to his face. Sparky was right. His glasses were definitely not where they should be.

Stanley's eyes stretched wide. 'Oh, no!' he said, rather too loudly for a watching-a-film-at-the-cinema voice. Several people in the row in front turned to look at him.

'I've left them in the toilet!' he added more quietly.

Sparky's eyebrows shot upwards. 'Why?' she said.

Two more people in the row in front turned. 'Sshhh!' they hissed.

'But why, Stanley?' Sparky whispered. 'Why did you take your glasses off in the cinema toilet? Who does that?'

'I splashed them when I washed my hands. So I took them off and put them down to get some paper to dry them. And then I got distracted because someone else came in and I forgot to pick them up when I left...' He paused. 'I need to go back and get them. Stay here.'

Sparky didn't appreciate being told to 'stay here' yet again. Especially not by someone who had foolishly left his glasses in a public toilet. But she slumped back into her seat and returned her attention to the film.

It must have been a good ten minutes later before it suddenly occurred to her that Stanley should have been back by now. After all, the toilets were only along the corridor. She and Mrs Smart usually used them at least once during a cinema trip. What could be holding him up?

Sparky looked away from the screen and peered into the darkness of the aisle. She willed the doors at the back to swing open, just enough to let someone the size of a Stanley back in.

'Please, God,' she said inside her head, 'please let the doors open **right... now!**'

The doors didn't.

Sparky didn't really expect God to magically open the doors and make Stanley appear, complete with his glasses on his face where they should be. But at least talking to Him helped her to feel that she wasn't alone. If Stanley didn't come back for the next half an hour, God would be right beside her.

And she was pretty sure that God would never be so absent-minded as to leave His glasses (if He wore glasses) or anything else in a toilet.

Another five minutes passed. By now, Sparky had lost track of the film completely. She'd never be able to fill in the gaps for Stanley. She could hardly remember who was who, let alone who'd done what.

All she could think of was her missing brother and the possibility that... *she might never see him again!*

In most situations, it's important to do as you're told. Even when it's an older brother doing the telling. Sensible instructions tend to be given to keep you safe.

But at times like this, when your older brother has vanished into thin air (or down a toilet) and it's entirely possible that they need YOU to save them – well, that's a completely different kettle of fish.

Sparky had 'stayed here' for as long as she could. Now it was time for her to spring into action.

She jumped out of her seat and scurried along the dim aisle to the doors. She pushed on one of them and slid through the gap, the door swinging closed behind her.

Once outside the studio, she looked both ways along the corridor. There was no sign of Stanley. In fact, there was no sign of anyone. No one to ask: 'Excuse me, have you seen a fairly tall boy – well, fairly tall for 13, anyway – who looks quite grown up – well, quite grown up for 13, at least – with short, straight hair, and who may or may not have been wearing glasses with dark blue frames that make him look a bit cleverer?'

Sparky rather wished she had a pair of glasses of her own. Stanley's seemed to have done wonders for his confidence and, just at the moment, she felt as though hers could have done with a boost too.

She started to make her way towards the toilets. They were just at the end of the corridor and round a corner. Finding them was easy-peasy. It was only as Sparky stood in front of them that she realised the next step in her plan to find Stanley was anything *but* easy-peasy.

There were two sets of toilets. As is usual in cinemas, shops, restaurants and in the street, one set was for

ladies and one set was for men. Normally, that didn't present a problem. Today, however, it did. Today, Sparky was a girl who needed to go into the men's toilets.

Hmm... she thought. *Now what?* And she hoped her powers of quick-thinking wouldn't let her down.

They didn't. *I know! I don't have to go in at all. I'll just put my face really close to the door and call.*

Sparky shuffled forward. In a quiet voice, she called, 'Stanley...? Stanley...?'

There was no sound; no movement from the other side of the door.

Maybe that was too quiet. I'll try again a bit louder...

'Stanley! Stanley, are you in there?'

Silence.

Sparky went to call again. But the door was suddenly whisked open. The movement was so quick, it made her jump.

'Eek!' she squeaked and leapt backwards.

The man who had opened the door jumped too: **'Aagh!'** Immediately, his face scrunched into a frown.

'What are you doing?' he asked.

'Nothing.' Sparky gave her head a sharp shake. 'Just... waiting for someone.'

'Right,' said the man, and he hurried away, still wearing his scrunched frown.

It was only as he disappeared round the corner that Sparky realised she'd missed her chance. She could have asked the frowning man to go back into the toilet and call for Stanley.

Bother, she thought.

Sparky was now faced with two choices: go and look for another man to call for Stanley in the toilets – or go into the toilets and call for him herself.

She decided that enough time had been wasted, so she'd

go in herself. In fact, she didn't even need to go in all the way. She could simply pop her head around the door – which she did, having quickly checked to make sure there was no one around to see.

'Stanley...? Stanley...?'

As far as Sparky could make out from a quick glance, the toilets were empty. But she leaned in a little further and called again.

'Stanley...?'

Stanley definitely wasn't there. No one was there. At least, not in the toilets.

'Can I help you?'

Once again, Sparky nearly jumped out of her skin.

One of the cinema attendants stood behind her. He wore a maroon shirt, part of the cinema staff uniform, and a name badge that said 'Rodney'.

Sparky recovered just enough to say, 'No, thank you... erm... Rodney... I was just... looking for my brother.'

And she scampered away. Back to the studio where she and Stanley had been watching the film.

The thing is, she thought as she scampered, *Stanley said he was going to the toilets to find his glasses. So if he's not in the toilets, then he must be back watching the film. It's the only explanation.*

Sparky wasn't sure she fully believed that it was the *only* explanation. But it was the only explanation she wanted there to be.

A little breathless from her scamper (not to mention the two shocks she'd just had), she stopped outside the studio doors and pushed her way through. She waited a moment for her eyes to adjust to the dim light. Then she walked down the aisle, keeping them fixed on the rows of seats.

One... two... three... four... five!

She was back. She knew she was back because she and Stanley had counted the rows on their way in, and they were in row five. On the end.

For one second, Sparky's heart leapt with excitement. There was someone in Stanley's seat, and that could only be Stanley!

'Stanley!' she cried.

As she did so, she realised that not only was there someone in Stanley's seat, there was someone in her seat too. And the seat next to that – which had been empty when she left.

At the sound of Sparky's voice, a cluster of faces turned to look at her. A cluster of faces that looked both surprised and annoyed at the disturbance.

And not one of them belonged to Stanley.

Sparky stared. The faces stared back.

Then, 'What are you doing in my brother's seat?' she demanded of the lady on the end. 'And what are you doing in *my* seat?' she added, with a hard look at the man who sat next to her.

'I'm sorry?' said the lady.

'You're in my brother's seat!' said Sparky. 'He's coming back, you know. He's only nipped to the toilet to get his glasses.'

Several people in the row in front had turned to see what all the commotion was about.

'Sshhh!' hissed a man.

'Yes, sshhh!' hissed a lady who sat next to him.

'I will not "sshhh"!' snapped Sparky. 'My brother, Stanley, and I have paid for our seats in this cinema and these people have stolen them!'

People in the rows further down now also turned to look.

Sparky might not have been quite so upset about the situation if she hadn't already been so extremely worried about Stanley.

'For one thing,' she went on, 'we've hardly been gone for any time at all, and for another – it's just rude!'

The lady and the man who seemed to be sitting in Sparky and Stanley's seats looked confused and rather put out.

'Well, I'm sorry,' said the lady, 'but you've obviously made a mistake. We've paid for our seats in this cinema too. *These* seats. Which is why we're sitting in them.'

'Absolutely right,' said the man. 'I don't know where your seats are but these are certainly not them.'

Sparky was growing crosser by the minute. 'If you don't give us back out seats *right now,* I shall go and get one of the cinema people, and *then* you'll be in **big trouble!**'

As Sparky heard the words tumble out of her mouth, she could hardly believe her ears. Perhaps she didn't need glasses to be as confident as Stanley after all.

'Excuse me, but – how old are you?'

The man in the row in front who had told her to shush had swivelled in his seat and now fixed her with a sharp gaze. Sparky gazed back.

'I happen to be nearly nine,' she said, 'but I really don't see what that's got to do with anything.'

'Oh, it's got a lot to do with everything,' replied the

man. 'Because to be allowed to watch this film, you have to be at least 15!'

Sparky was about to retort that she *was* allowed to watch this film because she was exactly the right age and, if anything, *he* was too old – when she happened to glance up at the screen.

The film that she and Stanley had come to see was an animation.

The film showing in this studio wasn't animated at all. This was a film with actors. Proper, human actors. Proper human actors in old-fashioned clothes – and one of them was crying.

'Oh...' said Sparky. 'Erm...'

'I think you might be in the wrong place,' said the man.

'Erm... yes,' Sparky replied. 'I think I might be too.'

She looked at the lady and the man who weren't in fact sitting in her and Stanley's seats because they were in an entirely different studio.

'Well...' she gulped. 'Sorry.'

With that, she turned to leave – and nearly walked straight into two cinema attendants who had appeared in the aisle behind her. Someone who'd been watching the film had gone to fetch them, because 'a little girl was being a nuisance'.

'Come with us now, please,' one of them said.

It was only when Sparky was on the other side of the studio doors in the brightly lit corridor that she recognised the man as Rodney. The lady with him wore a maroon shirt too. Her name badge said 'Brenda'.

'Hello, Rodney,' Sparky said. 'It's me again.'

'I can see that,' said Rodney. 'Now, just what exactly do

you think you're up to?'

Sparky bit her lip. She looked from Rodney to Brenda and back to Rodney. They both had very serious expressions on their faces. Neither of them looked in the mood for any nonsense. Especially not from a nearly nine-year-old girl who'd not only just been caught in a film she wasn't old enough to see, but had also, a short time before, been caught trying to get into the men's toilets.

There was nothing for it. She'd have to tell the truth and just pray that they would believe her.

Please, God, she murmured inside her head, *please let them believe me...*

And then Sparky said it...

'Rodney... Brenda... **I think my brother's been kidnapped!**'

Sparky sat on a not-very-comfy chair in the cinema office. It wasn't a very tidy office, probably because it was too small for all the furniture in it. Every surface was covered in folders or leaflets or lost property. To make room for Sparky to sit down, Rodney had moved the scruffy pile of papers and magazines that had been on the chair. They were now perched precariously on a shelf next to three dirty cups and a plate with a half-eaten doughnut on it.

Brenda was talking on the phone. Rodney had just returned from a thorough hunt of the toilets where Sparky said Stanley had left his glasses.

'There's definitely no sign of him,' he said, shaking his head. 'Or, I'm afraid, his glasses.'

Sparky didn't think she would cry. If she was going to cry, she was sure she would have already done so by now.

But all of a sudden, the thought of Stanley lost out there, somewhere, wearing his beautiful new blue glasses was too much for her. Her lower lip stuck out and began to wobble.

'Now, now,' said Rodney, 'let's not have any of that. He'll turn up, you'll see. I reckon he just popped outside for a breath of fresh air, bumped into a friend from school, and the pair of them are yacking their hearts out not far away, right this minute. Tell you what,' he added, 'how about an ice cream? Ice cream always makes things better. No charge.'

Sparky managed a smile. She wasn't sure whether she really wanted an ice cream. Not while she was so worried about Stanley. But Rodney had been so kind that she didn't like to refuse. Besides, once she actually had an ice cream, it might help her to think more clearly. She'd found ice cream to be helpful in that way before.

'Yes, please. Chocolate, please,' she sniffed.

'One chocolate ice cream coming right up,' Rodney said. He headed for the door. However, before he could open it, someone on the other side had pushed on it, nearly sending the surprised Rodney flying backwards, feet over head, across the corner of the desk.

Recovering his footing just in time, Rodney found himself face to face with another man. He was much younger than Rodney and also wore a maroon shirt. He had a name badge too, but Sparky couldn't read it properly from where she was sitting.

The man looked around as if he'd lost something

important.

'Has anyone seen my doughnut?' he said.

'Erm...' Rodney hesitated and glanced around.

'Is it a doughnut that someone's eaten half of?' asked Sparky.

The young man looked at her. He seemed surprised – partly to find a stranger in the office and partly because the stranger had spoken to him.

'No,' he said. 'No, the last time I saw it, no one had eaten any of it.'

'Oh,' Sparky replied, 'because there's a half-eaten doughnut on a plate over there.' She pointed.

The man stepped into the office and shuffled around Rodney to have a look. 'No, that's not mine,' he said, and peered at it. 'My doughnut was a whole one. I thought I'd put it behind the counter where I was selling tickets, but it's not there so it must be in here. It was in a paper bag. Unless that one's mine and someone else has had a go at it. Has anyone had a go at my doughnut?'

He threw Rodney an accusing glare. Rodney shook his head and rolled his eyes. Brenda took no notice because she was still on the phone.

The man shook his head too. 'I don't reckon that's my doughnut,' he said. 'I think mine's got lost.'

'Yes, well, the thing is, Gordon,' said Rodney, sounding cross, 'just at the moment we've got rather more important lost things to look for than your doughnut.'

'Have we?' Gordon scratched his head. 'What's that then?'

Before Rodney could answer, Brenda put the phone down. 'The police are on their way,' she announced.

Once again, Gordon's face looked surprised. 'The police?'

Brenda's eyes slid towards Sparky to see how she would take this news.

Sparky's shoulders slumped and once again her lower lip quivered.

'But that's a good thing,' Brenda added quickly. 'The police will find your brother – just like that,' and she snapped her fingers. 'Now then, I need to phone your parents.'

'Nooo!' Sparky jumped off the chair. She felt her heart speed up and begin to thump loudly. 'You can't phone them – you *can't*! They're both busy. They said we could come to the cinema on our own. They said Stanley was in charge.'

Sparky's eyes flicked from Brenda to Rodney. '*Pleeease* don't phone our parents! Mum'll never let us out on our own ever again. Not ever!'

'What's happened to your brother?' asked Gordon.

'If we knew that, he wouldn't be lost, would he?' Rodney snapped. He seemed to have no patience with Gordon. 'Look, if you want to make yourself useful, go and get a chocolate ice cream for the little girl.'

Sparky frowned. *Little girl?* She wanted to say, 'I'm *actually* nearly nine.' But Rodney was trying to be kind and she didn't want to upset him.

Gordon didn't make himself useful and go and get Sparky an ice cream. 'Do you mean he's disappeared?' he asked. 'Your brother?'

Sparky nodded and sank back onto her chair.

'Listen, darling,' said Brenda, 'I really do need to phone your parents. I can't not let them know what's going on. Especially with the police coming.'

'But can't we just try to find him first?' Sparky pleaded.

'You said the police would find him. If they find him then Mum and Dad will never need to know.'

'I think they'd *want* to know,' said Rodney. 'I know I'd want to know.'

Gordon glanced at him. 'I didn't know you had children.'

Rodney tutted. 'I haven't. But if I had, I'd want to know.' He looked back at Sparky. 'And your parents certainly wouldn't want you to be sitting here all upset and on your own.'

'How come your brother's disappeared?' Gordon asked Sparky.

Rodney turned to him. 'Gordon, please, just go and get the girl a chocolate ice cream.'

'But what happened?' Gordon persisted. 'Did he just leave? Where did he go?'

Sparky let out a heavy sigh. 'He went to the toilet to get his glasses. He left them in there by mistake. We were watching a film.'

'Which studio were you in? Number four?'

Sparky blinked at him. 'I think so.'

'Makes sense. It's the only kids' film we've got on this week.'

'Oh.' Sparky was impressed. Gordon was obviously a quick-thinker like she was. Although she had to admit that her own powers of quick-thinking had been seriously blunted by the vanishing of Stanley.

'So, he went to the toilet and he didn't come back?' Gordon was beginning to sound like a policeman himself. 'And which toilets did he leave his glasses in?'

That was a funny question. There was only one set of toilets that Sparky knew about. Down the corridor and round the corner from the studio where she and Stanley had been watching the film.

'*The* toilets,' Sparky answered. 'You know, the round-the-corner ones.'

'Right, makes sense,' Gordon said again. He nodded his head in a thoughtful way for a moment. Then he looked at Rodney. 'But did you check the others – just in case?'

Sparky noticed that Rodney had the same expression on his face that Mrs Smart sometimes wore. Mrs Smart wore this particular expression when she was interrupted while trying to plan maths lessons for school. In fact, Sparky half expected to see one of Rodney's eyes begin to twitch.

'I didn't need to check the others, Gordon,' Rodney muttered, 'because the little girl told me which toilets her brother had left his glasses in.'

'Makes sense,' Gordon said for the third time. There was a pause before he added, 'But don't you think we ought to check anyway?'

Sparky stood up. 'You mean, there are *other* toilets?'

'Toilets all over the place here,' Gordon replied and gave her a wink. 'You just have to know where to look.'

Rodney seemed to be growing more irritated by the second. 'Who do you think you are – Chief Inspector Gordon of the local constabulary? I checked the *right* toilets and the boy wasn't in there. Now are you going to go and get the little girl a chocolate ice cream or am I?!'

This time, Sparky barely noticed the 'little girl' remark. Her heart had begun to beat even faster. Gordon had suddenly given her a glimmer of hope. If Stanley couldn't be found in one set of toilets, maybe – just maybe – they might find him in another.

'Please, Rodney,' she said, 'please may we go and look

in the other toilets?'

Rodney's head swung round. He didn't look happy.

'It's not that I don't think you did a brilliant job of looking for Stanley in the round-the-corner toilets,' Sparky said, 'because you did. No one could have searched those toilets better than you. It's just... well, what if I made a mistake? What if the toilets I thought were the *right* toilets have actually been the *wrong* toilets the whole time?'

Rodney's head drooped and he threw up his hands. 'Fine. *Fine.* Gordon and I will go and look in the other toilets. Although why he'd still be in there after all this time is anyone's guess.'

'Oh, thank you, Rodney!' Sparky wanted to give him a hug, but she wasn't sure he'd want one, so she didn't. 'May I come too?'

Brenda stepped forward. 'No, wait a minute. I need to phone your parents. You need to give me their phone number. I think you should stay here while I talk to them.'

Sparky looked with desperate eyes from Brenda to Rodney to Gordon. 'But if we find him, there'll be no need to phone them. And then they won't have to worry.'

Gordon also looked at Brenda and Rodney. 'Makes sense,' he agreed – which is exactly what Sparky had hoped he would say.

Brenda folded her arms. She eyed Gordon as if she thought this whole situation was his fault. Then, 'Five minutes,' she said. 'If you're not back here in five minutes, I'm coming to get you. And then we *are* phoning the little girl's parents.'

Sparky, Gordon and Rodney left the office and walked

briskly towards another set of toilets. A set of toilets Sparky knew nothing about.

Sparky didn't speak. Not out loud anyway. But inside her head she said over and over and over again: 'Please, God, *please* let Stanley be in the other toilets!'

They passed the ticket counter and headed upstairs towards studio four. On the way, Sparky spotted the round-the-corner part of the corridor with the toilets where she thought Stanley had left his glasses. Nearby was the door to studio three.

That's where I made my mistake! thought Sparky as she remembered how she'd walked back into the wrong studio. *I took a door too early...*

They had almost reached the opposite end of the corridor when, suddenly, Sparky saw them. Toilets! Toilets she knew nothing about!

'If your brother's going to be anywhere,' said Gordon, 'I reckon it'll be here.'

'Do you, Gordon?' replied Sparky.

She wanted to believe him. She'd never wanted to believe anything so much in her life.

'Go on, then, Chief Inspector Gordon,' grunted Rodney. 'Don't keep us in suspense. Go and have a look.'

Sparky clasped her hands together in front of her. 'Can I have a look too?'

'Well... not really,' Rodney answered. 'It's the men's.'

'Tell you what,' said Gordon, 'Rodney can hold the door open with his foot. Then you'll be able to see from out here.'

'Can I indeed?' said Rodney.

'Oh, thank you!' squealed Sparky.

Gordon pushed open the door. Rodney slid his foot in

front of it to hold it in place.

'Is there anyone in here?' Gordon called.

No answer.

Sparky felt as if her heart had just tripped over itself.

Gordon followed the line of cubicles with his eyes. The second-last door was closed. He walked towards it and, as he stopped, he put out his hand to give it a push.

The door didn't move.

He glanced back at Sparky and Rodney and pointed at the locked door. Then he gave it a knock. 'Is there anyone in this cubicle?'

Again, no answer.

Sparky couldn't stop herself. At the top of her voice, she shrieked, 'Stanley! Stanley it's Sparky – are you in there? Oh, *please* be in there!'

There was silence. Nobody moved. Nobody said another word.

Until a quiet voice from behind the locked door spoke. 'I'm here, Sparky.'

Sparky's eyes lit up in a way they had never lit up before. She began to jump up and down, clapping her hands together at the same time. **Never in her whole life had she been so glad to hear her brother's voice.**

And never again would a cinema toilet *ever* seem so exciting.

✻ ✻ ✻ ✻

'So,' said the policeman, 'let me just run back over this.' He glanced down at the notes he'd made.

Mr Smart stood next to him with a pained expression on his face.

OLICE

Stanley and Sparky stood there too. Stanley had one bare foot. He held the dripping shoe and soggy sock that the foot should have been inside, in his hand. He tried not to look at the small crowd that had gathered, who were keen to see what the commotion was.

'You went to the toilet, but when you arrived back in the studio you realised you had left your glasses on the washbasin bench in the toilets,' the policeman continued. 'So you went back to retrieve them. (Police people tend to use big words like 'retrieve'. It means 'fetch' or 'get something back'.)

You then decided to use the toilet – again – during the course of which you became trapped inside a cubicle. You tried various things, such as pulling and jiggling the bolt, but you were unable to open the door.

Next, you attempted to get into the next-door cubicle in order to make your escape from there. This meant having to climb up onto the toilet. However, once in position, you lost your balance and one foot slipped into the toilet bowl. This foot somehow became wedged and you were unable to pull it out.

Several people came in and out of the toilets during the time that you and your foot were trapped. But you decided not to call out for help as you felt somewhat embarrassed. Which isn't at all surprising.'

The policeman looked up from his notes and stared at Stanley. 'Is that about right?'

Stanley gave his head a gloomy nod.

'You were finally released,' the policeman finished, 'by one of the cinema attendants, Mr Gordon Floss. Mr Floss broke down the door, which in turn knocked you over and the force of this resulted in the extrication of your foot from the toilet bowl.' (Yes – 'extrication' is another of those police-person-type words. It means 'removal' or 'freeing' – just in case you're interested.)

'Throughout the whole course of these events, no injuries were sustained by any person or persons.'

Police people certainly do talk funny, thought Sparky. *Or perhaps that should be 'police persons'...*

'Nothing to add?' asked the policeman.

This time, Stanley gave his head a gloomy shake.

'Good,' said the policeman. 'I'll go and get all this typed up.'

Mr Smart had a gloomy look about him too. 'Would you like us to come to the police station?'

'No, no,' said the policeman. 'I've got everything I need. Sorry you ended up with a wet foot, Stanley. Still, all's well that ends well, eh? And look on the bright side – now you'll have something fun to tell your friends about at school on Monday morning.'

For the first time since the policeman had arrived, Stanley lifted his head, and stared at him. Sometimes, he seriously wondered about grown-ups and their idea of fun. Exactly what part of this afternoon could be called 'fun'? What planet would you have to live on to think that *falling into a toilet and getting your foot stuck in it* was 'fun'?

'Right, then,' said the policeman, 'I'll be off. I've got your phone number if I do need to speak to Stanley again, Mr Smart. But I don't think I will.'

He turned away and walked to the police car that was parked outside the cinema.

The three Smarts watched him go.

'Can we go home now?' Stanley muttered. 'I want to go to bed for the rest of my life. And I've got a really cold foot.'

'Don't go to bed for the rest of your life, Stanley,' said Sparky. '**I'd miss you**. Besides, that policeman was right about one thing. "All's well that ends well," he said. And it is.'

'That's easy for you to say,' said Stanley. 'You're not the one who spent almost the entire afternoon with your foot down a toilet...'

☆ ☆ ☆ ☆

At bedtime, Sparky knocked on Stanley's door.

'Stanley? It's Sparky. May I come in?'

Stanley's voice answered. 'I suppose so.'

When Sparky walked in, she found Stanley sitting up in bed. He wasn't looking at his laptop or reading a book. He was just sitting.

Sparky sat down beside him.

'I was really worried about you today, Stanley. *Really* worried.'

'Thanks,' said Stanley.

'I thought I might never see you again.'

'Did you?'

'Yes. It made me realise that, although you're quite annoying and grumpy most of the time, and you do go on about the weather an *awful* lot – I'd actually really miss you if you weren't here.'

'Would you?'

'Yes. And Gordon was such a hero. If it hadn't been for him, I really might never have seen you again.'

Stanley sighed. It was just about the heaviest sigh

Sparky had ever heard him sigh before.

'Can we stop talking about it now, please?' said Stanley. 'I'm trying to forget this day ever happened.'

'The thing is though, Stanley,' Sparky went on, 'I've been thinking. I prayed and prayed that God would help me to find you. And to start with, I didn't think He was going to. Because I kept asking and I kept not knowing where you were.

But then, all of a sudden, He sent Gordon. Gordon had lost his doughnut. That might seem like nothing, but if Gordon hadn't lost his doughnut, he might never have come into the office to look for it. And if he hadn't come into the office to look for it, he might never have met me. Then, he might never have known you were missing.'

Stanley chewed his lip. 'Good,' he grunted.

'But don't you see, Stanley?' said Sparky. 'Today, I think Gordon was like an angel. An angel God sent to rescue you because I asked Him to help. I asked Him and He heard me. That's how much God loves you, Stanley. He sent someone to help us find you who knew exactly the right place to look.'

Stanley stopped chewing his lip and seemed thoughtful.

'And anyway, God doesn't care that your foot got stuck in a toilet,' added Sparky, 'so why should you? God will always love you just the way you are – whatever happens to either of your feet.'

Stanley gave another sigh. This one was far less heavy. 'I'd quite like to have been Gordon, though. I'd quite like to have been the hero.'

Sparky smiled. 'You'll always be my hero, Stanley.'

Stanley smiled too. 'Thanks, Sparky,' he said.

STORY 3

The bee in Mrs Smart's bonnet

When Sparky walked out of school at the end of the week, she was surprised.

It was usually Grandad Bagg who came to pick her up.

It was Grandad Bagg she always looked out for at the school gates.

It was Grandad who was the first to hear about Sparky's day: how well (or how not-so-well), for instance, she'd done in a spelling test; what mark she'd got for her story about a unifrog (basically a frog with a horn on its head – she'd got the idea from Sissy's cuddly pink unicorn); how many times tables she could now recite before she got stuck; and what had happened when her teacher, Mr Barber, had unfortunately sneezed during quite a tricky science experiment.

Yes, Grandad was 'the norm'. So, as she walked out through the school gates, it wasn't the sight of Grandad that surprised Sparky. Not in the least. Nor was it the sight of Barbara.

Barbara was Grandad's moped. She was purple with an orange seat and Grandad loved her very much. Going out for trips on Barbara reminded him of his young days and a motorbike he'd once owned called Esmerelda.

Sometimes, he'd take Barbara to meet Sparky from school. But Mrs Smart wasn't ready for Grandad to give Sparky a ride yet. So they'd walk home together and Grandad would push Barbara along the road at the edge of the pavement.

'Hello, Grandad. Hello, Barbara,' said Sparky. She always included Barbara in any form of greeting.

(Now for the surprise part. Well, it was a surprise for Sparky, anyway.)

'Hello, Mrs Pringle!' Sparky was so surprised to see Mrs Pringle that she stopped dead on the pavement. 'What a surprise to see *you* here.'

Mrs Pringle lived a few doors down from Grandad on the same street, at Number 12.

Sparky noticed that Grandad's spare moped helmet dangled from Mrs Pringle's finger. As if Sparky's eyes weren't wide enough already, they went a little bit wider.

'Have you been riding on Barbara?' she asked.

'I have, Sparky,' replied Mrs Pringle. 'And what a lovely little mover she is.' Mrs Pringle beamed.

'I hope you don't mind Mrs Pringle joining us on our walk home,' said Grandad. 'It wasn't planned. I just ran into her.'

Sparky's eyes couldn't stretch any wider, but they did fill with alarm. Grandad and Barbara were sometimes a bit wobbly.

'You ran into her, Grandad? On Barbara?' Sparky gasped. 'Oh, Mrs Pringle, I do hope you're not hurt!'

Really, though, Mrs Pringle looked far too cheerful to be hurt.

She and Grandad Bagg glanced at each other and Grandad chuckled.

Mrs Pringle shook her head. 'I'm not hurt in the slightest, Sparky – although it's very kind of you to be concerned. No – your grandad didn't run into me on Barbara. We ran into each other. You know – we met by chance. *That* sort of running into.'

'Ohhh!' said Sparky. *Sometimes the way people talk is very confusing,* she thought.

They all set off for Grandad's house, with Grandad pushing Barbara along the road. When they arrived, Sparky expected Mrs Pringle to say goodbye and head off down the street for Number 12.

She didn't.

'How about a cup of tea?' asked Grandad.

'I'd love a cup of tea,' said Mrs Pringle. 'I'll just pop home and pick up some of my special milk.'

Special milk? thought Sparky. *I wonder what's special about Mrs Pringle's milk...*

That's when she remembered. Grandad had once said to her that there was a lot she didn't know about Mrs Pringle. Perhaps Mrs Pringle's special milk was part of her mystery.

Grandad rolled Barbara into the garage, then unlocked his front door.

'Grandad,' said Sparky, as he marched into the kitchen to put the kettle on, 'why is Mrs Pringle's milk special? Does it come from special cows?'

'It doesn't come from cows at all,' said Grandad. 'It's almond milk. It comes from almonds.'

'From *what*-monds?' asked Sparky.

'*Al*monds,' Grandad repeated. 'You know – nuts.'

Sparky had begun to think the day couldn't get any more surprising, but she was wrong. How could anyone *milk a nut*? She pictured Mrs Pringle holding a small nut over a glass and squeezing it. In the picture in Sparky's head, nothing came out.

And even if it did, thought Sparky, *how ever many nuts would you need to squeeze to fill up a whole glass with milk? Mrs Pringle must be very clever. And have magic nut-milking fingers.*

'Grandad?' asked Sparky.

'Yes, Sparky.'

'Doesn't Mrs Pringle like the milk cows make?'

'It's not that she doesn't like it,' Grandad answered.

'It's that she's... erm... what's the word...? Allergic.'

Al-monds? All-er-jick? (*All-er-jick* was how Sparky pictured the word in her head. It's actually spelt the way Grandad said it – allergic. In case you're interested...) Really! How many more difficult words were going to pop out of Grandad's mouth as if they weren't difficult at all?

Sparky folded her arms across her chest. 'Which means?'

'Which means,' said Grandad, 'it's not very good for her. She has a bad reaction to it.'

Sparky unfolded her arms instantly. 'Ooh! What sort of reaction?'

In the picture in Sparky's head, Mrs Pringle suddenly threw the nut she'd been milking up into the air. Her face turned purple, her short, curly hair flopped down dead straight, and she began to run around and make barking noises, a bit like Mr and Mrs Obi's dog, Minnie, next door.

Grandad thought for a moment. 'Do you know, I've never asked her what sort of reaction. I just know that she has one.' He frowned and his big, bushy eyebrows sank down over his eyes. 'To be perfectly honest, I'm not sure I'd *want* to know!'

'Wouldn't you?' said Sparky. 'I would. I like to know everything about everyone.'

'Do you now?' Grandad replied. 'I'd never have guessed. Now, let me see. I wonder if there's any cake left in the tin?'

* * * *

Grandad didn't stop for a cup of tea when he dropped Sparky home later. He gave crochet lessons down at the community centre and had a few crochet patterns to sort through for his next class.

'How was school today, Sparky?' asked Mrs Smart.

'It was very good, thank you,' said Sparky. 'But the most interesting thing I learnt wasn't in school. Did you know you can be *all-er-jick* to milk from cows?'

'Yes, I did,' answered Mrs Smart. 'How did you find out about that?'

'Because Mrs Pringle from Number 12 on Grandad's street can't have cows' milk. So that she can have something to put in her tea, she has to milk nuts.'

'Mik nits, mik nits,' sang Sissy.

Sissy sat on the floor by the back door with her shape-sorting toy. The idea with a shape-sorting toy (as you're sure to know) is to match the shape with the same shaped hole. That way, you can easily post the shape through the hole so that it drops into the little bucket underneath.

However, that was far too painstaking for Sissy. Sissy preferred to skip the shape-matching part and try instead to force the shapes into the *wrong* holes. This was, of course, impossible and meant that a lot of banging was involved.

Mrs Smart stood at the kitchen sink and began to prepare the vegetables for dinner. 'You know, Mrs Pringle probably doesn't milk the nuts herself. You can buy almond milk in shops. But, how did you find out that she can't have cows' milk?'

'Grandad told me,' Sparky replied. 'But I'd have found out anyway.'

'Would you?'

'Yes. Because Mrs Pringle had to go home to milk some nuts when Grandad made her a cup of tea.'

Mrs Smart stopped part way through scrubbing a carrot. 'Sorry...?' She turned to look at Sparky. 'So Mrs Pringle dropped in after school?'

'Oh, no,' said Sparky. 'Mrs Pringle was with Grandad when he came to pick me up with Barbara. He ran into her.'

Mrs Smart dropped the carrot into the sink. It landed with a soft thud. Far softer than the noise Sissy was making.

'Grandad ran into Mrs Pringle on Barbara?' One wet hand smacked itself onto Mrs Smart's forehead as she gasped. 'Is she all right? What happened? Did she call the police? I told you he was too wobbly on that thing. You are *never* riding on the back of it, Sparky, and that's final. Did she have to go to hospital? I mean, why didn't Grandad say something when he dropped you off? **Oh, this is *awful*!**'

Thanks to Sissy's shape-banging, neither Sparky nor Mrs Smart heard Mr Smart arrive home from work. He appeared suddenly in the kitchen, with a towel draped around his neck. For once, he wasn't hot and sweaty. More importantly and most unusually after a day at work, thought Sparky, he didn't smell.

'What's awful?' asked Mr Smart.

'It's Dad!' cried Mrs Smart. 'He ran Mrs Pringle over on Barbara! You know – Mrs Pringle from Number 12!'

Mr Smart pulled the towel from his neck and threw it over a chair. 'Did he? Is she all right?'

Mrs Smart stepped forward, grabbed the towel and threw it into the washing machine. 'I've no idea. I've only just found out from Sparky that it happened. Dad didn't say a word. He's going to have to get rid of that thing. He can't be allowed to be a danger to other people, let alone himself.'

Mr Smart went to the washing machine and pulled out the towel Mrs Smart had just thrown inside. 'Well, let's not jump to conclusions. We don't know what happened yet. Maybe Mrs Pringle stepped off the pavement in front of him.' He dropped the towel onto the chair.

Mrs Smart swung round to Sparky. '*Did* Mrs Pringle step off the pavement in front of Grandad? Was it her fault? Oh, why am I asking you? You weren't even there.' Mrs Smart gabbled on. 'And I'm jolly glad you weren't or you could have been hurt too! I mean, was it just Mrs Pringle? Was anyone else involved? Oh, my goodness, perhaps we should phone the police!'

You may be wondering why Sparky hadn't already leapt in and explained that Grandad Bagg hadn't run into

Mrs Pringle on Barbara. That Grandad and Mrs Pringle had, in fact, met by chance – *that* sort of running into.

But, as you've probably gathered, once Mrs Smart gets going, very little can be done to stop her. And Sparky had learnt something important during her eight (nearly nine) years: there were times when there was *simply no point* in interrupting. A misunderstanding was one of those times. Once Mrs Smart had made up her mind about something, it was better to wait and let her pour everything out (and there was usually a lot of pouring), until she stopped. Then, and only then, might there be enough space for someone to step in and tell her what had *actually* happened.

Sparky waited for the space. And then she did explain what had actually happened.

Instantly, Mrs Smart threw up her hands. (It's a good job she wasn't still holding the carrot. Who knows where that might have ended up.)

'Well, why didn't you say that in the first place, Sparky?' she grumbled. 'Letting me get hold of the wrong end of the stick like that. Honestly!'

Mrs Smart picked up the towel that Mr Smart had replaced on the kitchen chair and tossed it back into the washing machine.

'Erm... why do you keep doing that?' asked Mr Smart, and went to get it out again.

'Because it's dirty and sweaty,' said Mrs Smart. 'It needs washing.'

'But it's not dirty and sweaty,' Mr Smart replied. 'Neither am I, not today.'

Mrs Smart clicked her tongue against her teeth.

'Well, you could have said so. If you'd said so, I wouldn't have put it in the machine in the first place. No wonder Sparky struggles to give me the right information. She takes after you!'

'Arter-noo... arter-noo...' sang Sissy. *Bang, bang, bang!*

Mrs Smart returned to scrubbing carrots, but rather more vigorously than before.

'So,' she went on, 'is this the first time Mrs Pringle's been in for a cup of tea after school?'

'Yes,' Sparky replied, 'because it's the first time I discovered you can be *all-er-jick* to milk from cows. When Grandad and Mrs Pringle go out on their adventure, Mrs Pringle's going to have to take her special milk with her.'

Another carrot thudded into the kitchen sink. Mrs Smart turned sharply. 'What "adventure"?'

'Oh, it sounds *brilliant* – I wish I could go!' Sparky's eyes gleamed. 'They're going on a steam train and then on a boat down the river, and then on a steam train again. It's going to take a whole day. Grandad says it'll be a "trip down memory lane" because the boat part will remind him of when he used to be a ferryman.'

Mrs Smart's wet, carroty hands landed on her hips. They made little damp patches on her t-shirt but she didn't seem to notice. 'Hang on a minute, Sparky – are you telling me that Grandad and Mrs Pringle are going out together for the whole day on a steam train and a boat?'

Sparky nodded. 'And then another steam train, yes. I told Mrs Pringle that I'd love to go on a boat, but Stanley can't because he gets seasick. He gets sick on boats even when they're not on the water. Do you remember that time he climbed on the ark down at the play park, Dad, and –'

'Yes, thank you, Sparky. I remember it vividly, as it happens, and it's something I'd really rather put behind me,' Mr Smart interrupted. This was just as well because, when it comes to seasickness (or any other type of sickness), nobody wants to hear about it. Especially not in a book.

'But we don't know anything about this Mrs Pringle,' said Mrs Smart. 'How can Grandad go out for the whole day with someone we don't know anything about?'

'That's all right,' Sparky replied, 'Grandad knows lots about her. He says Mrs Pringle's lived at Number 12 for nearly four months and they're always running into each other.'

Mrs Smart looked a little as you might look if you were about to enjoy a bar of chocolate, only to find that someone else has already eaten half of it. 'Are they indeed? And how are they going to get to this train-and-boat-and-train day thing?'

'Mrs Pringle's going to drive them both in her car,' Sparky answered.

Mrs Smart made a face. 'Well, I don't like the sound of that. She might be a terrible driver and have no sense of direction.'

'Oh, they won't get lost,' said Sparky. 'Mrs Pringle's got a sat nav. She knows how to use it and everything. Anyway, guess what? Mrs Pringle used to be a taxi driver so I think she must know exactly what she's doing.'

'Really?' Mrs Smart's lips were pressed together in such a tight, straight line, it was a wonder she could talk at all.

'Yes. And Grandad says it's very nice that they can be friends with each other, because, after all, God didn't make us to be on our own.'

'But he's *not* on his own,' said Mrs Smart. 'He's got us.'

Mr Smart dropped his towel on the back of a chair and sat down. 'It's nice for him to have friends of his own too, though.'

Sparky sat down next to Mr Smart. 'And God is so clever! He's found Grandad the *perfect* friend.'

Mrs Smart sat down next to Sparky. 'Has He? And what's so *perfect* about Mrs Pringle?'

Sparky grinned. 'Mrs Pringle likes singing to tomatoes just like Grandad does. Because do you know what she did? She asked Grandad if she could sing to *his* tomatoes!'

Mr and Mrs Smart exchanged a glance.

'Did she?' said Mr Smart. 'And what did Grandad say?'

'Grandad said yes, of course! And he didn't even mind that Mrs Pringle didn't sing opera.'

When Grandad Bagg sang to his tomatoes, it was usually something grand from an opera. Grand and rather loud. He listened to opera on the radio too, and he'd been to see quite a few operas performed in theatres. It was his favourite type of music.

'Well, what did Mrs Pringle sing?' asked Mr Smart.

'It was a song from a group that she really liked when she was young,' Sparky answered. 'They were called "The Beatles" – but not spelt with two "e"s like the creepy-crawly sort of beetle. Which is good because Grandad wouldn't want creepy-crawly beetles in his greenhouse. Mrs Pringle says the group, "The Beatles", has an "a".'

Mrs Smart got up from her seat and began to pace backwards and forwards. The carrots, and indeed the rest of dinner, were completely forgotten.

'Mrs Pringle asked lots of questions about tomatoes too,' Sparky went on. 'She wanted to know if Grandad feeds them; when they'll be ripe; how big they'll grow and how much water they'll need. I think Mrs Pringle must be planning to grow some tomatoes of her own.'

Mr Smart chuckled. 'Well, I think it's rather sweet. Grandad's got a tomato buddy. And he must be very fond of Mrs Pringle if he let her sing songs by "The Beatles" to them. You know how he feels about opera.'

Mrs Smart was still pacing. She glanced at Mr Smart and shook her head.

'No,' she said. She now looked as you might look when you're about to enjoy a bar of chocolate, only to find that someone else has scoffed the lot. 'No, there's something not right about this. What kind of person asks to sing to *someone else's* tomatoes? And what kind of person sings "The Beatles" when they know those tomatoes are used to hearing opera? It doesn't make any sense.'

'I think it sounds fine,' Sparky replied. 'I ask Grandad if I can go down to the greenhouse and sing with him most times I'm there. And sometimes I sing to his tomatoes on my own. But I'm not very good at opera, so I sing the first thing that comes into my head – which might be from a TV advert or something. Grandad doesn't mind at all. His tomatoes don't seem to mind, either.'

Mrs Smart stopped pacing and sat down. 'Yes, well, he wouldn't mind what *you* sing, would he? You're Sparky and he loves you. But this Mrs *Pringle*' – she spoke the name as if it wasn't a real name at all – 'she's got no business being in Grandad's greenhouse. And she's certainly got no business singing something he wouldn't want sung to his tomatoes. But you know Grandad – he'd have been far too polite to say so. And as for all those questions,' Mrs Smart rattled on, 'well, I think it's just rude.'

She sat back in her seat, folded her arms across her chest and began to chew at her lower lip.

'So, what are you saying?' asked Mr Smart.

'What I'm saying is,' Mrs Smart answered, 'there's something funny going on.'

'Funny gong... funny gong...' chanted Sissy. *Bang, bang, bang!*

Sparky stared. 'Something funny like what?' Mrs Pringle was already a bit of a mystery because of her nut-milking. Could there really be something even more mysterious about her than that?

'I don't know,' said Mrs Smart. 'I really don't know. But if you ask me,' and she glanced from Sparky to Mr Smart and back again, 'that woman's up to something...'

* * * *

Sparky sat up in bed and waited for Mr Smart to come in to say good night. She could hear Sissy, who was fast asleep in the other bed, doing her slow, deep, fast-asleep breathing.

Up to something... she thought. *What does someone look like who's 'up to something'?*

Sparky began to imagine all sorts of possible up-to-something looks.

She supposed that an up-to-something person might wear dark sunglasses. Then, if their eyes looked shifty because of what they were up to, no one would be able to see them. Sparky had never seen Mrs Pringle wearing sunglasses.

She supposed an up-to-something person might wear a pretend smile all the time that was too big for their face. No one would think they were up to something if they looked bright and happy, would they? Mrs Pringle seemed like a cheerful sort of person, but her smile wasn't too big. It was just the right size.

Sparky supposed an up-to-something person might wear a disguise so that they didn't look like themselves at all. Then, if they did something they shouldn't do, no one would have a clue who had done it. But Sparky had only ever seen Mrs Pringle look like Mrs Pringle.

She'd like to think that an up-to-something person might have a cloak that made them invisible. That way, they could disappear underneath it and get up to all sorts of mischief without anyone even noticing. But Sparky was fairly sure cloaks that made you invisible weren't real. Even if they were, they were probably very expensive and hard to get hold of. Not at all the sort of thing Mrs Pringle might have hanging in her wardrobe.

'Dad?' whispered Sparky when Mr Smart came in. She had to whisper so as not to wake Sissy. 'Do you think Mrs Pringle's up to something?'

'No.' Mr Smart shook his head. 'Your mum's just very protective of Grandad, and that's understandable. But I think, if he's found himself a girlfriend, then good for him.'

'A girlfriend?!' Sparky was so shocked, she almost forgot to whisper. 'Do you think Mrs Pringle is Grandad's *girlfriend*?'

Dad gave a quiet chuckle. 'She might be, mightn't she? But whatever type of friend she is, I think it's very nice for him. And for Mrs Pringle. So, if Mum wants us to get to know her a bit, that's fine by me.'

Mrs Smart, however, didn't want the family to get to know Mrs Pringle a bit. She wanted them to get to know her *a lot*.

'We're going to be detectives,' she had said at dinnertime. The carrots had finally been scrubbed and cooked. 'We're going to find out everything we possibly can about Mrs Pringle. What she used to do, where she used to live, whether she has any family, what she does now and what she's planning to do.'

'Isn't that a bit nosey?' said Stanley. 'If someone wanted

to know all that about me, I'd think they were nosey.'

Sparky munched on a jacket potato. 'You won't have to worry about that, Stanley,' she said. 'I don't suppose anyone will ever want to know all that about you.'

'It's not nosey,' said Mrs Smart. 'It's all about looking after Grandad and keeping him safe.'

Mr Smart sighed. 'I see what you mean, but... the few times I've talked to Mrs Pringle, she seems very nice. She lent us her roof box when we went on holiday. I really don't think this is something we need to worry about.'

'And anyway, Mum,' said Sparky, 'you're always saying we should look for the best in people. That we need to try to see the good things in them that God sees. I'm sure God sees lots of good things in Mrs Pringle. Shouldn't we try to see them too?'

Mrs Smart bent down to pick up the spoon Sissy had just dropped on the floor – for the third time. She took it to the sink and rinsed it under the tap – for the third time. 'We *are* trying to see the good things in Mrs Pringle. We'll just be able to see them a lot more clearly when we know more about her.'

'More pout-er,' Sissy said.

She took the freshly rinsed spoon from Mrs Smart – and dropped it back on the floor.

'So...' said Mrs Smart.

'So...' said Grandad.

'So...' said Mrs Pringle.

It was Saturday morning. The Smart family all sat in the lounge with Grandad Bagg and Mrs Pringle, who they'd invited over for coffee. Mrs Pringle had come prepared with a jug of almond milk – much to the disappointment of Sparky, who was rather hoping to catch a glimpse of some real-life nut-milking.

Stanley sat in his own special place on the sofa. As the oldest of the junior Smarts, he felt he deserved his own special sofa seat. But he wasn't happy. Today, he really didn't care whether he got to know Mrs Pringle or not. He'd heard that there might be a thunderstorm some time over the weekend. So the only place he wanted to be was in his bedroom, where he could keep track of it on his laptop.

'Well, I must say,' said Mrs Pringle, 'it's very kind of you all to invite me round for coffee. I feel honoured.'

Mrs Smart laughed. Not a real laugh. One of those pretend sorts of laugh that always comes out too loudly.

The kind of laugh, thought Sparky, *that means you're up to something.*

'Oh, there's no need to feel honoured,' Mrs Smart said. 'We just wanted to get to know you a bit better, Mrs Pringle.'

'Please,' replied Mrs Pringle, 'call me Verity.'

Sparky blinked. 'Does Grandad call you Verity?'

'I do indeed,' said Grandad.

'My real name's Sabrina. Did you know?' asked Sparky.

'I did, as a matter of fact,' Mrs Pringle answered. 'And I think it suits you perfectly.'

Sparky beamed. 'I think your name suits you perfectly too.'

'So...' interrupted Mrs Smart. She was impatient to start collecting information about Verity Pringle. 'Tell us all about yourself, then – *Verity*.'

Mrs Pringle look at Grandad. '*All* about myself? I think that might take rather a long time. I *am* 70!'

'Well,' said Mrs Smart, 'just start with a few things. I hear you used to be a taxi driver.'

'I did, yes. My husband and I had a taxi business where we used to live. We both used to drive the cars.'

'And where was that exactly – where you used to live?'

'Cornwall,' replied Mrs Pringle. 'And we had a lovely view of the sea.'

'Did you?' Sparky couldn't imagine anything more exciting. 'I'd *love* to live by the sea!' Her shoulders slumped a little. 'I'd like a dog too, but I don't think that's going to happen either.'

'I love Cornwall,' said Mr Smart.

'So do I,' agreed Grandad.

'I've never been,' grunted Stanley.

'I might be getting a dog,' said Mrs Pringle.

'Really?' Sparky's smile seemed to stretch from one ear to the other. Whatever they found out about Mrs Pringle now, she didn't care. Mrs Pringle liked dogs. As far as Sparky was concerned, that meant she was wonderful.

'It must have been lovely living by the sea,' said Mrs Smart. 'Whatever made you decide to leave and come here?'

Mrs Pringle smiled. 'It *was* lovely. I was very happy there. It just didn't seem quite so lovely after my husband died.'

There was a pause.

'Oh... Well, of course not...' Mrs Smart smiled back. A warm, kind smile, with nothing pretend about it. Just for a moment, Sparky thought that perhaps Mrs Smart wasn't being a detective anymore.

She was wrong.

'So, when did you leave Cornwall?' asked Mrs Smart.

'Eight years ago,' answered Mrs Pringle. 'I moved all the way up to Scotland.'

'Wow!' squealed Sparky, and even Stanley's ears pricked up.

'I love Scotland,' said Mr Smart.

'So do I,' replied Grandad.

'I've never been,' sighed Stanley.

Sparky's eyes danced. 'Have you ever seen the Loch Ness Monster? Grandad's been up to Scotland on holiday and he's never seen it.'

Mrs Pringle chuckled. 'Do you know, I never have. And I used to keep my eyes peeled for him every day.'

Sparky wasn't sure why anyone would want to peel their eyes. She was sure hers worked perfectly well with their peel on.

'So you came here from Scotland?' Mrs Smart was quickly on to her next question.

'Oh, no,' replied Mrs Pringle. 'After Scotland, I went to Wales.'

'Did you?' Sparky cried. 'Mrs Pringle, you really have lived *everywhere*!'

Mrs Pringle gave another laugh. 'Well, not quite *everywhere*, but I've made my way around a bit. I suppose, since I lost my husband, I've become a little restless. I try somewhere out for a while and then I move on.'

'I love Wales,' said Mr Smart.

'So do I,' said Grandad.

'I've never been,' muttered Stanley.

'Oh...' Mrs Smart clasped her hands together in her lap. 'So, you might move on from here soon too?'

Grandad finished his coffee and put his mug down on the little table in front of him. 'So many questions! You sound like a detective!'

Mrs Smart was taken aback. So much so that, when she opened her mouth, nothing came out because she didn't know what to say.

'Oh, I don't mind,' said Mrs Pringle. 'I rather like being able to talk about myself. I'm flattered you're all so interested.'

'Oh, we're interested all right,' said Mr Smart, and he gave Mrs Smart a sideways glance.

Mrs Pringle finished her coffee and placed her mug next to Grandad's on the little table. 'And as for moving on from here, I think I might be getting a bit old for much more gadding about. Besides, I'm rather hoping I might have found somewhere to settle.'

She gave Grandad a quick look, which Grandad returned with a smile.

Mrs Smart, who had just taken her last mouthful of coffee, almost choked. Mr Smart had to pat her on the back, and Stanley and the sofa got caught in the spray.

'Sorry,' gasped Mrs Smart. 'Went the wrong way,' and she thumped her own chest.

Mrs Pringle swiftly pulled out a handkerchief to help with the mopping up. Stanley pulled away as she began to dab at his t-shirt.

'Don't worry, Stanley,' she said, 'this is clean. I'm not the sort of person to dab at someone with a dirty hanky!'

As soon as Mrs Smart had recovered, and Stanley and

the sofa had been thoroughly mopped with Mrs Pringle's hanky, Mrs Smart returned to her detective work.

She discovered that Mrs Pringle had never had any children of her own; that before she was a taxi driver, she'd been a doctor's secretary; that she couldn't ride a bicycle; that her favourite vegetable was beetroot; and that she didn't like aeroplanes.

Mrs Smart also discovered the rather surprising fact that Mrs Pringle didn't especially enjoy gardening.

'Oh,' said Mrs Smart. 'But Sparky told us how interested you were in how Grandad grows his tomatoes. I thought you must be growing some of your own.'

Mrs Pringle shook her head. 'I'm certainly very fond of tomatoes,' she said. 'But I'm no gardener myself. I wouldn't know one end of a bean pole from another.'

'Oh...' Mrs Smart's eyes narrowed just a tiny little bit. It was such a tiny little bit that Mrs Pringle probably wouldn't have noticed. Sparky, however, noticed straightaway.

'So...' Mrs Smart continued, '...if you're not interested in gardening, then why were you asking Grandad so many questions about his tomatoes?'

Mrs Pringle looked at Grandad and smiled. 'Because they're very impressive,' she said, 'and I just wanted to know what his secret is. You see, I happen to know he's won first prize in the garden show with his tomatoes for three years running.'

Grandad's bushy eyebrows danced upwards in surprise. 'Do you now?' he said.

'Anyway,' Mrs Pringle added, 'I need to know how you care for your fruit and vegetables if I'm going to look after them next weekend.'

There was silence.

'Sorry?' said Mrs Smart.

'I'm going up to London next weekend,' said Grandad.

'Are you?' replied Mrs Smart. 'It's the first I've heard of it.'

'I'd not got round to mentioning it. I managed to get a ticket to the opera. I'll only be gone a couple of nights. But Verity has very kindly insisted on keeping an eye on things while I'm not here. Just in case we get a burst of hot weather.'

'I don't think we will,' said Stanley. 'I've looked at the forecast for next weekend, and I don't think we will.'

'I see.' Mrs Smart sat forward on the sofa and crossed her arms. 'But, *we* normally keep an eye on things when you're not there.'

'I know. It's just that you're always so busy.'

Mrs Smart shook her head. 'It's no problem at all. You're only round the corner.'

'I know,' Grandad said again. 'But Verity's made the offer to save you the bother, and I'm very happy to accept it.'

There was another silence.

'I love London,' said Mr Smart.

'So do I,' said Grandad.

Stanley nodded. 'Me, too. When I'm a TV weather person, that's where I'm going to live.'

Mrs Smart said nothing.

'Right, then,' and Mr Smart got to his feet. 'Who's for another cup of coffee?'

* * * *

The following Thursday, just after Grandad had dropped Sparky home from school to Priory Park, a leaflet was pushed through the letterbox.

Mrs Smart picked it up. 'Annual Garden Show,' she read. She glanced at the colourful pictures of flowers, fruit and vegetables. 'Goodness me, is it that time of year already? Grandad *will* be pleased.'

Sissy stood in the kitchen doorway. She held a banana in one jammy hand and there was jam all around her mouth. 'Goodiss ee,' she said, and wiped jam on her nose.

'Grandad will have lots of tomatoes to show,' said Sparky. 'I wonder if he'll win first prize again?'

'It depends, doesn't it?' Mrs Smart dropped the leaflet

on the hall table and went to fetch Sissy. She lifted her up and placed her back down on a chair at the kitchen table. Sissy spent much of her time being sticky. The trick was to try to keep the stickiness in one place.

'Does it?' replied Sparky. 'But Grandad's tomatoes look brilliant.'

'They do now, Sparky. But you're forgetting, Mrs Pringle's looking after them this weekend. Who knows what they'll look like when he gets back on Monday?'

Sparky's face frowned. 'I'm sure Mrs Pringle won't hurt Grandad's tomatoes, will she? She knows how important they are to him. And he's away for hardly any time at all. What could she do that's so bad in hardly any time at all?'

'I don't know.' Mrs Smart sighed and shook her head. 'But she's not a gardener. She said so herself. I really do wish Grandad would just let us keep an eye on everything the way we usually do when he's not there.'

'You still think Mrs Pringle's up to something, don't you?' Sparky's frown hadn't moved.

Mrs Smart didn't answer. She just shrugged her shoulders. As she did so, she realised there was a smear of jam on one of them. She went to the kitchen sink and was about to wipe the sticky patch away with the dish cloth, when she stopped. Her mouth fell open. She dropped the cloth and whirled around.

Sparky's frowning eyebrows shot up in surprise. 'What, Mum?!'

Mrs Smart stared at her. 'I know what this is!'

'What what is?' Stanley appeared in the kitchen doorway.

'*This!* Mrs Pringle!' shrieked Mrs Smart. 'I know what

she's up to!'

She pushed past Stanley, rushed to the hall table and grabbed the Garden Show leaflet.

'This!' she shrieked again and held it up. As she did so, one eye began to twitch. Not just once or twice. It twitched over and over, and showed no signs of stopping.

Sparky and Stanley exchanged a glance.

Mrs Smart was beside herself. 'The Garden Show! It's on in two weeks!'

'We know that,' said Stanley. 'It says so on the leaflet.'

'But two weeks, Stanley! It's a bit of a coincidence, isn't it?' Mrs Smart began to pace up and down. 'First, Mrs Pringle asks all sorts of questions about Grandad's tomatoes. Next, she mentions how Grandad has won first prize at the Garden Show for his tomatoes for the last three years. Then she offers to look after his tomatoes for him while he's away for the weekend.'

Stanley and Sparky looked blank. Even Sparky's famous quick-thinking couldn't keep up.

Mrs Smart stopped pacing and threw her hands in the air. 'Don't you see? Mrs Pringle wants to spoil Grandad's tomatoes so that she can enter her own in the Garden Show and win first prize instead!'

Sparky and Stanley stared at Mrs Smart and tried to take this in. Sissy, who couldn't care less about anyone's tomatoes, had begun to draw swirly jam patterns on the table with her banana.

'But,' said Sparky at last, 'Mrs Pringle doesn't grow tomatoes. Remember? She doesn't grow anything. She says she doesn't know one end of a bean pole from another.'

'Yes – that's what she *says*,' said Mrs Smart. 'But just because that's what she *says*, that doesn't mean that's the way it really is!'

Stanley looked serious. 'Well, what can we do? Shall I go round to Grandad now and tell him?'

'No!' Sparky cried. She couldn't get Mrs Pringle's kind, cheerful face out of her mind. 'We can't say anything to Grandad because we don't know if it's true! And he really likes Mrs Pringle. He'd be so upset.'

'He'll be more upset if she ruins his tomatoes.' Mrs Smart chewed on her thumbnail. 'But, you're right. We can't tell him. Not until we've got some hard evidence.'

Hard evidence? Sparky thought. Clearly Mrs Smart was back in detective mode. ('Hard evidence' means 'actual proof', by the way – just in case any of this is confusing.)

'Anyway,' Mrs Smart continued, 'there's no point telling Grandad. He'll never believe us. He only ever sees the good in people.'

Grown-ups can be so confusing sometimes, thought Sparky. *I thought we were* supposed *to see the good in people – like God does.*

'Right,' said Mrs Smart. Her eye twitches began to calm down as she started to make a plan. 'First things first. We need to have a look in Mrs Pringle's garden. If she's growing tomatoes out there, we'll know we're on the right track.'

Sparky wasn't convinced. *Grandad always says that the best way to know if you're on the right track or not is to talk to God about it,* she thought. *And if we forget to talk to God, then finding the right track can be a lot harder.* The trouble was, Mrs Smart was so busy worrying about

Mrs Pringle being 'up to something', Sparky began to think that she must have forgotten about talking to God...

* * * *

The following afternoon, the day Grandad was leaving for his weekend in London, he picked Sparky up from school as normal. But instead of going back to Grandad's house, they went straight to Priory Park. A short while later, Mrs Smart arrived home from work with Sissy.

'I am so glad it's nearly the holidays,' she said as she dumped her bags on the kitchen table. 'This has been *such* a long term.' She smiled at Grandad. 'Now, then, what time's your train? We mustn't be late to the station.'

'Didn't I say? I don't need to trouble you for a lift after all,' Grandad replied. 'Verity's offered to take me.'

Mrs Smart's smile faded. 'Mrs Pring – I mean, Verity – doesn't need to do that. I'm quite happy to take you.'

'No, no,' Grandad said. 'Verity thought it would save you the bother so it's all arranged.'

'I see.' Mrs Smart looked put out. 'Well, would you like us to come and pick you up from the station on Sunday or is *Verity* doing that too?'

Grandad looked at Sparky and winked. 'I'd *love* you to come and pick me up on Sunday. I shall look forward to hearing all about your weekend.'

'And we'll look forward to hearing all about your opera,' said Sparky. 'Maybe you'll learn some new songs to sing in the greenhouse.'

'Maybe I will,' said Grandad.

'And you're sure there's nothing you want us to do in the garden while you're not here?' asked Mrs Smart.

'Because it's absolutely no trouble.'

'Nope,' said Grandad. 'It's very kind, but Verity has it all under control.'

'Yes, I'll bet she has,' muttered Mrs Smart.

Sparky and Mrs Smart, with Sissy in her arms, stood on the doorstep and waved Grandad goodbye.

When Sparky had gone to bed the night before, she had talked to God about everything. She'd told Him how Mrs Smart thought Mrs Pringle was up to something. She'd asked Him to help Mrs Smart see the good in Mrs Pringle. And as she'd drifted off to sleep, a thought had popped into her head. Thoughts sometimes did pop into her head after she'd talked to God. She always hoped those thoughts were God talking back to her. Sometimes she was sure they were.

In last night's thought, it occurred to Sparky that maybe Mrs Smart was afraid. Maybe she was afraid that now Grandad had Mrs Pringle, he'd want to be with her rather than with the family.

Maybe she was afraid Grandad wouldn't love them so much anymore.

Now, as they turned to go back in the house after Grandad had gone, Sparky looked up at Mrs Smart. 'You don't need to worry, Mum,' she said. 'Just because Grandad has a girlfriend, that doesn't mean he'll stop loving us.'

Mrs Smart glanced down at her – which wasn't as easy as it sounds. Sissy had a crayon in her fist and was trying to poke it up Mrs Smart's nose.

'I know that,' she said. 'What a funny thing to say, Sparky. Anyway, we don't know that Mrs Pringle is

Grandad's girlfriend.' She put Sissy down. It was the only way to avoid a nasty crayon-up-the-nose incident. 'What we do know, however, is that she will soon be taking Grandad to the station. And you know what that means, don't you?'

'Grandad won't miss his train?' answered Sparky.

Mrs Smart raised her eyes. 'No! It means Mrs Pringle will be out. Which gives us the perfect opportunity to nip round and have a look in her back garden...'

* * * *

An hour later, Mrs Smart picked up the phone and rang Grandad. He didn't answer.

'Good,' she said. 'They must have gone.'

Ten minutes later, Mrs Smart and Sparky, with Sissy in her buggy, stood outside Grandad's house. They rang his doorbell just to make sure he'd left.

'But what will we say if he hasn't?' asked Sparky. This whole situation was making her feel extremely uncomfortable.

'He has left,' said Mrs Smart. 'His train is at half past six. If he's still at home now, he'll miss it.'

When Grandad didn't answer the door (as Mrs Smart knew he wouldn't), she led the way to Mrs Pringle's house at Number 12. She and Sparky peered over the front garden wall. Sissy wasn't high enough up in her buggy to be able to peer over anything.

Mrs Pringle's front garden was small and neat, but a bit dull. There were no flowers or bushes. There were certainly no tomatoes. In fact, the only growing thing was the grass.

'You see?' said Sparky. 'Mrs Pringle said she wasn't a gardener. And that garden definitely belongs to someone who isn't a gardener.'

Grandad's front garden had pots of lavender and geraniums along the path, and a red rose that climbed around the front door.

'Yes, well, that's probably what she wants us to think,' Mrs Smart replied. 'We need to see in the back garden.'

'Gack cardin,' said Sissy, who could only see the wall.

There was an alleyway that ran along behind Number 12 and all the other houses in the row. It was private, so only people who lived there were allowed to use it. Each back garden had a gate in the fence that led out into the alleyway.

'All I want is a quick peek,' said Mrs Smart, as she turned into the alley and pushed Sissy briskly towards the back gate of Number 12.

Sparky trotted along behind. 'We're not supposed to be here, Mum,' she hissed.

Mrs Smart took no notice. 'It's all right,' she said in a low voice. The last thing she wanted to do was draw any attention. 'Grandad lives here and we're family. So it's not really private to us.'

The fences at the edges of the back gardens were quite tall, with tall gates to go with them. You couldn't see over the top. The gates looked like part of the fences too, so you couldn't see through them. And they were all exactly the same. The only way to tell which house you were behind was to count them.

Mrs Smart had been counting. When she got to gate Number 12, she stopped. 'This is the one.'

She put her hand over the top of the gate and felt around for a bolt. 'There must be a way to get in,' she muttered. 'I mean, what's the point of a gate if it doesn't open?'

There was no bolt or latch, however. These gates, it seemed, were only meant to be opened from the garden side. Probably to stop intruders getting in. Intruders like the Smarts.

Mrs Smart looked around. 'I need something to stand on. Then I'll be able to see over the top.'

There was nothing. The alleyway was empty – apart from the Smarts themselves and a plump tabby cat that had just appeared at the far end.

Mrs Smart suddenly dived forward and lifted Sissy out of her buggy. 'Hold onto her hand, Sparky, and don't let her run away,' she said. Then she kicked off her shoes.

Sparky's eyes opened wide in horror. 'Mum! You can't stand on Sissy's buggy!'

'Can't I?' said Mrs Smart. 'Why not?'

She had already pushed it up against the fence.

'But you'll break it, Mum!'

'Just hold the handle, would you, please?' said Mrs Smart. 'To make sure it doesn't tip.'

Have you ever been in a situation that has got out of hand? Sparky, in her nearly nine years, had been in several. They had usually got out of hand because she'd said something she shouldn't have said or done something she shouldn't have done. And quite often, it was Mrs Smart who had to help her get out of the out-of-hand situations.

However, the situation she was in right now was about

to get out of hand *because* of Mrs Smart. So, for Sparky, this was rather an odd turn of events.

Very carefully, Mrs Smart put one foot on the seat of the buggy. She reached up with her hands and placed them on top of the fence. Once she had some sort of balance, she pulled herself up, placing her other foot on the buggy seat as she did so.

Sparky hung on to the buggy's handle with one hand as tightly as she could. With the other, she held firmly on to Sissy's hand.

Unfortunately, seeing Mrs Smart standing on *her* seat in *her* buggy, Sissy began to tug at the hand Sparky held. 'Sissy buggle!' she whined.

'Sshhh!' Sparky shushed, which made no difference at all.

'Sissy buggle! Sissy buggle!' Sissy said, over and over.

Between pulling herself up and balancing in the buggy, Mrs Smart had at last managed to get her head above the top of the fence.

And her eyes bulged.

The garden she gazed into was full of fruit and vegetables. There were rows of onions and lettuces, cabbages and carrots, potatoes and cauliflowers, and runner beans scrambling up tall poles. There were fruit bushes too – blackcurrants and redcurrants. One of them might even have been a gooseberry.

Everything was neat and orderly, and almost as well planned as Grandad's garden.

And then, she spotted them – through the glass of a small greenhouse: tomatoes! Large ones and small ones, smooth and round, and all turning shiny and red in the summer sunshine. They were beautiful. Exactly the sort of

tomatoes you might enter in a garden show!

Mrs Smart gasped. Yes, indeed, the person who lived here not only knew all about gardening – they were also very good at it.

But the thing was, the person who lived here – the person who kept this wonderful garden – was *not* Mrs Pringle.

Mrs Smart realised this, partly because the man who popped out of the greenhouse with a broom was most certainly *not* Mrs Pringle. And she realised it partly because Mrs Pringle had just stepped into the garden of the house next door – with Grandad.

This was the wrong garden of the wrong house.

Sadly for Mrs Smart, although she couldn't see right into Mrs Pringle's garden from Sissy's buggy, Mrs Pringle and Grandad could see her all too clearly.

So could the man with the broom. 'Oi!' he shouted. 'What do you think you're doing?'

At the same moment, despite Sparky's best efforts, Sissy escaped. She did so with a 'tuggle-twisty' – a sharp tug and a twist of the hand that meant she was now free in the alleyway.

'Sissy buggle!' Sissy said and plonked down in the buggy seat on top of Mrs Smart's feet.

Not knowing quite where to look first, Mrs Smart's head whipped around. The sudden movement meant that she lost her balance.

As the buggy tipped, Mrs Smart squealed, 'Oh, no!' Seconds later, she lay sprawled on the concrete floor of the alleyway.

Luckily for Sissy, as the buggy tipped over, she landed

on Mrs Smart.

Unluckily for the tabby cat, it got caught under the tipping buggy. Nothing too serious, and it was out again within moments. But as it streaked away, it yowled at the top of its voice and wore a rather startled expression on its face.

'Mum!' screamed Sparky.

'Stella!' shouted Grandad.

'Oh, my goodness!' shrieked Mrs Pringle.

Mrs Pringle and the man with the broom pulled their gates open at exactly the same time. Mrs Smart could see them leaning over her.

She saw Grandad too. She heard Sparky say, 'Grandad, I'm so sorry!'

Then she closed her eyes and hoped with all her heart that none of it was real. That it was all just a very bad dream...

* * * *

Mrs Smart sat on Mrs Pringle's sofa next to Sparky. She stared out through the big window in the lounge onto a bare back garden. Just as in the front, there was grass and nothing else. Not a vegetable in sight.

Mrs Smart sipped a cup of tea that was far too sweet. It had three heaped teaspoons of sugar in it. Mrs Smart didn't usually take sugar in her tea but Mrs Pringle said she needed it. For the shock.

'We've all had a shock,' said Grandad. He sat opposite in an armchair, Sissy on his knee.

Mrs Pringle stood by the door with her arms folded.

'Why didn't you go to London, Grandad?' asked Sparky.

It wasn't often that Grandad didn't have a twinkle in his eye. In fact, it was almost never. But he didn't have one now. 'The train was cancelled. I could have got the next one but I thought, no. I'll go in the morning instead.'

Mrs Pringle didn't look her usual cheerful self either. 'I'm sad you thought I was up to something,' she said, and she looked hard at Mrs Smart. 'Very sad indeed.' She glanced at Sparky. 'I'm extremely fond of your grandad. He's been so kind to me. I wouldn't hurt him for all the world.'

Mrs Smart put down her mug. 'I know, Mrs... Verity. And I'm sorry. It was just that you were so interested in how Dad grew his tomatoes. And you were so keen to check on them while he was away. I suppose...' She hesitated. 'I suppose I *wanted* you to be up to something because...'

Her voice trailed off.

Sparky reached out and held Mrs Smart's hand. 'It's like I said before, Mum. Because you were afraid Grandad might not love us so much if he had a girlfriend.'

Grandad's eyes darted towards Mrs Pringle.

Mrs Pringle's eyes darted towards Grandad.

And Grandad chuckled.

'Verity isn't my girlfriend!' he said. Suddenly, his twinkle was back.

'No, I most certainly am not!' Mrs Pringle giggled. And suddenly, she looked cheerful again.

'We're just friends,' said Grandad. 'Good friends. Close friends. Because sometimes being friends like that is all you need.'

Mrs Smart's eyes filled with tears. 'I'm so sorry, Dad. I'm so sorry Mrs... Verity. Sometimes I get such a bee in my bonnet and I just can't seem to let it go.'

Sparky imagined Mrs Smart in a big, buzzing hat. *Grown-ups do say funny things,* she thought.

'You're a wonder, Sparky, do you know that?' Mrs Smart gazed at her. 'How could you possibly know how I was feeling? I don't think even *I* knew how I was feeling.'

Sparky thought for a moment. 'Well,' she said, 'I know that you like to look for the good in people, because that's what you tell us to do. And that's what God wants. So I couldn't understand why you didn't want to see the good in Mrs Pringle.'

'Missy Cwingoo,' said Sissy.

Sparky turned to Mrs Pringle. 'I think there's lots of good in you, Mrs Pringle, by the way.'

'Oh, you sweet thing.' Mrs Pringle perched down on the arm of Grandad's chair. 'That's very kind of you, Sparky, I must say. I think there's rather a lot of good in you too.'

'Anyway, I decided to tell God all about it,' Sparky continued. 'And after I'd told Him, I listened for Him. Then...' She shrugged her shoulders. '...I just sort of knew.'

Mrs Smart leaned over and gave her a hug.

Sparky sighed. 'Telling God didn't stop you thinking Mrs Pringle was up to something, though, did it, Mum? And it didn't stop you falling off Sissy's buggy and hurting yourself on the concrete.'

Mrs Smart hugged her tighter. 'None of that's your fault, Sparky Smart. Not one bit. All of this happened because even though you talked to God – I didn't. And I rather wish I had.'

Sissy fidgeted on Grandad's knee. He spread out her arms and made aeroplane noises. Sissy laughed and made some aeroplane noises of her own.

Grandad looked across at Mrs Smart. 'I'll always love all of you exactly the same,' he said. 'However many girlfriends I have and however many buggies you fall off. You do know that, don't you, Stella?'

'Yes, Dad. I do.' Mrs Smart nodded. 'I just forgot for a bit.'

'Good,' said Mrs Pringle. 'Because I promise you, I'm not trying to steal him away. Girlfriend indeed!' She giggled again. 'The very idea!'

Sparky pulled away from Mrs Smart and sat upright on the sofa.

'Just so you know, though,' she said, 'if you ever *did* want to be Grandad's girlfriend, Mrs Pringle, we wouldn't mind. And, Grandad, if you ever *did* want to be Mrs Pringle's boyfriend, we wouldn't mind that either. Because we can see the best in both of you, just like God can. Can't we, Mum?'

Mrs Smart wiped her teary eyes. 'Yes, Sparky. Yes, we most definitely can.'

Join the Smart family and the other residents of Priory Park for more fun!

THE CRINKLY COUSINS AND OTHER MISHAPS	THE PURRING WOMBAT AND OTHER MISADVENTURES	THE SCHOOL FETE FIASCO AND OTHER CALAMITIES
ISBN: 978-1-78259-825-1	ISBN: 978-1-78259-826-8	ISBN: 978-1-78259-929-6

All of the books in the **Sparky Smart from Priory Park** series are available from **cwr.org.uk/shop** or from your local Christian bookshop.

Have fun with God every day!

You can have a great time reading the Bible every day, and learn more about being God's friend! Join the Topz Gang on their adventures, with codes and puzzles to solve and prayers to pray. You can even get a subscription for the whole year!

Visit **cwr.org.uk/shop** or a Christian bookshop for more information.